LAST
STOP

JESSICA CAGE

ISBN-13: 978-1-7364885-2-2

I dedicate this book to Nicole... throughout it all. You have been there, supporting me, pushing me and being real with me when others seemed afraid to be. You are truly my rock and so much of Josephine is you. Strong, determined, and proud. Love you, girl!

Embrace your gifts!

TABLE OF CONTENTS

LAST STOP

"Last stop, exit in the rear!"

       I'd heard the conductor yell out the announcement so many times I dreamed about it. The days that the older man wasn't there to call out the end of the line, I missed him and the voice that had long since dropped to the lowest level of baritone.

       The loose flesh beneath his neck jiggled above his collar as he sang his tune. The last stop was my stop. On a typical night, as I approach my destination, the last stop on the last train, I was the only one left on board. Only once a week there was also a young boy who, judging from the overstuff duffle bag he carried with him, was a track star.

       Most people in my area knew him because his face was often plastered across the sports section news outlets. They'd dubbed him a future Olympic star. Every time I saw him, I smiled knowing that when the doors opened, his father would be there waiting for him.

       Each time I witnessed his welcoming, I wished, hoped, wondered what it would feel like to have someone waiting for me on the platform. But as the bells chimed, and I stepped out on the platform, there was no one. Just the warm night's breeze and a flickering light that always seemed to be moments from going out, yet it continued to hold on.

When I thought about it, that light was a perfect comparison to life. We were all just flickering lights, waiting for that last surge of electrical impulses before we faded to black. My more morbid side often reared its ugly head. There was no one there to welcome me, to walk me to my car and ride the ten blocks from the platform to my apartment. No one who would feel happy to know I'd made it home safely.

"Last stop, exit in the rear!" The conductor yelled it again. As if the added octave was necessary. That night, it was just me. He knew it, but he called it out all the same. Some days I appreciated it. It made me feel less pathetic, like perhaps there was someone else out there waiting for the train, or someone else who had drifted to sleep while riding along.

But on a bad day, when the world took a shit on my existence, it had just the opposite effect. It was like being at a restaurant full of couples and the hostess yells out, 'Party of one!' You'd sulk over to your table and pray that no one was watching, but you'd feel their eyes on you.

I stepped off the train and onto the waiting platform. The old conductor nodded, tilting his cap to me, and I return the gesture. That was our thing. We never spoke, just a head nod and on a good day, a soft smile. I turned away as the doors slid shut and the train pulled out of the terminal. Last stop.

The platform had seen better days. The damn thing was barely holding together. Apparently, the city saw no need to perform any type of repairs or maintenance. They hardly did any work on it. When they did, it was half assed patchwork that only insured the damn thing didn't collapse.

They left this place to wither away because there just weren't enough people who cared. Most people either drove their commute into the city or remained local for work. The lack of passengers meant not only did the platform get neglected, but the schedule got cut as well. You could only catch this train at this platform a few times a day, and the train only waited a whopping ten seconds before shooting off in the opposite direction.

No one was going to come running for it. Last train, last stop, either you were there when it arrived, or you found another way.

2

LAST STOP

The train's whistle faded off in the distance behind me. The old wood creaked beneath my feet as I walked towards the exit that would take me to the parking lot where my lonely car waited for me. As usual, as I walked, I said a prayer asking whatever entities that watched over me to let the things start up one more time.

My car needed a long list of repairs that I had been most effective at ignoring. The check engine light had been on for nearly two months. And no, I was not proud of that. I kept saying I would take it in to the shop. I rationed this major act of neglect with the fact that I didn't drive the car that much. Just to and from my apartment, to and from the last stop on the train.

Next to the old flickering light, was a battered old bench that no one sat on because rumor had it, a man died there. Right on its faded-out wood. It happened about ten years before I started riding the train, the random death of Edward Hill, forever unexplained.

As far as I knew that bench had been sitting there untouched ever since. I don't know how much stock I put into the story. This tale of a lost soul tied to a bench, the reason the light flickered but never goes out, just seemed like a far reach. Why would a ghost hang around an old rundown train station? What was the point? There was nothing there.

I guess I never was like most people. The idea of apparitions terrified them; it was the boogie man coming to get them. Most people thought of the afterlife as something to hold on to. Hope that when this life is over, there is more.

I never wanted there to be life on the other side. I didn't want to have to deal with more of the monotony. An eternity of it, in bright white light or flesh dissolving flames. I hoped to one day close my eyes, fall asleep, and that's it. It would simply stop. Last stop, nothing further, no return ticket. The coward's exit, some would call it.

The wood creaked louder, reminding me to send another pointless letter to the city in hopes of repair. I considered that they may have decided to wait it out, let the thing die on its own. The platform would fall, and my stop would no longer be the last stop. That would mean either driving further into town or taking the bus. And with my schedule I'd be on the bus late at night when it would be packed with nothing but crack heads and crazies. I'd look up places to purchase a taser after emailing the city.

I was just about to pass the bench, thoughts of Edward leaving my mind and being replaced by more things added to my shopping list, when my purse strap snapped. I froze in my frustration, took two deep breaths to calm my spirit because I didn't need my blood pressure to build, and then bent down to gather my things.

Of course, everything spilled out of the bag including the lip gloss that was two shades too light for me. It was an emergency buy when I realized my lips had been as dry as the Sahara just before a major presentation at work. I thought I had everything and was ready to get off my knees when I caught the flash of something shining underneath the bench.

The metal was hard to see with the flickering light and as I reached for it, I had a sensation of dread. This is when I should have retracted my hand, got the hell up and went home. That is exactly what I should have done. That is not what I did.

THE LOCKET

I dangled the moon shaped locket over the cup of jewelry cleaner, hoping I'd be able to restore it. If it was worth something, I could use the profit to fund that taser purchase or at the very least get enough to replace my purse. I cursed under my breath when I thought of how much I loved that purse.

It was my mama's. One of the last things I had of hers and there'd be no more to get because she passed away. There was no longer the overstuffed closet full of forgotten accessories for a broke daughter to rummage through. No potential replacement for the bag that would hold such sentimental value, or a nag fest about how I had just destroyed a perfectly good purse.

My mother was a nut about her bags. She took better care of them than most people took care of their children. Each one could have been twenty years old, but they all looked brand new. *'Nothing says more about a woman than the condition of her handbag.'* She would often scold me as she was scooping one of mine up off the floor.

It had been two years since I lost my mother. There was a virus going around and like thousands of others, she got it. A ton of people got it; a ton of people died. My mama's name was just another on the list to flash across the bottom of the screen of the nightly news. That moment haunted me. Reading her name underneath two newscasters talking about the local fair. I remember it, her name, Trudent Massey.

If you asked her, it wasn't the prettiest name around and she made everyone called her Trudy, as if that was any better. But there it was right under the word, bold print, all caps **EPIDEMIC**.

I closed my eyes for a long time after that, trying to erase that image. That couldn't be my last memory of my mother. Every time I thought of her, that couldn't be the first thing to come to mind. But there it was, clear as day in my memory two years later.

She would have had no problem restoring this old thing. I really missed her. I dropped the locket in the cup, giving up my effort. It hit the bottom with a thump and splashed the cleaner on the table. Frustrated with myself, I wiped up the mess and decided the best thing for me to do was take a shower and get to bed.

It was an enjoyable night outside, but it was hot and sticky inside my apartment. Of course, my air conditioner went out right before a heat wave hit Chicago. Not only that, thanks to the last bout of storms, my only functioning window barely opened.

That's the life of a studio dweller. But hell, it was mine. All my own and I was proud of that. Creaky floorboards, thin walls, and a leaky faucet, and it was all mine. I remembered the day I moved in. I was so happy not to have to return home after college. I hadn't planned on spending three years here. I crossed my fingers that soon I would be out of the slums.

The shower was refreshing, as expected. The second I stepped out, of course it was like I never got in. Beads of sweat formed on my brow faster than the water could dry from my skin. I toweled dried my hair, glad that I'd chopped it all off. To be in that heat with the long locs I had just a year before would have been maddening.

Cutting my hair had been an emotional journey. It was another thing that connected me to my mother. She loved to do hair; it was how she made ends meet. When I was a child, I was her test subject. If I could say nothing else, my shoes and clothes may have been worn down, but my hair was always the best in class.

Girls often tried to become friends with me not because of my

6

athletic prowess, or my artistic flair, but for a chance at a free hair styling by my mother, something she never actually did. Friends came and went.

I wasn't exactly the social butterfly. Even if I had wanted to keep them around, they would have all gotten bored and left, eventually. I didn't really understand girls. I grew up with a family full of male cousins. Even as an adult, I looked at them and sometimes wonder why women were the way they were. Total disconnect for me.

The heat was an annoyance, but it was one of the few things left that really made me feel alive. The sticky feeling of my skin was a response to something real. It told me I hadn't slipped away during the countless hours logged behind the desk of my job. I doubted I would notice if I had. That job was like a death in its own right. Except death has no timecard to punch.

I turned the small box fan on. It would only circulate the heat, but at least it would create something of a breeze. I got dressed in my usual lounge attire no matter what the weather, shorts and a tank top. The rumbling sensation in my stomach reminded me I had foolishly skipped lunch at my part-time gig in order to finish a report that they informed me just a few minutes after submitting it was unnecessary. The job, however monotonous, was just a steppingstone because I'd finally landed an opportunity of a lifetime.

I was a photographer, nature was my muse, and I had just landed a huge account working with a magazine that featured none other than our mysterious Mother Earth. It took over a month of pitching and test shots and then of course negotiations before I got it, but I was in. *The wonderful life of a freelancer.* At least that is how I thought of it.

I knew that starting out, freelancing would be a hassle, a total pain in the ass, but it was worth it. This was my shot, not only to get my work seen around the world but also to step into another tax bracket. It meant I could move further into town, not be the last stop, and leave my crummy day job in the dust. I hated punching the time clock and was done helping someone else make their dream come true while mine withered away.

I turned on the oven and took out the beat-up baking pan from the cabinet. I hummed happily as I rubbed the sides and bottom of the pan with olive oil. There were two marinated chicken breasts waiting for me in the refrigerator. It was rare that I actually remembered to prep before I headed out to work. Once I got the chicken going, I dropped some chopped veggies into the steamer and reheat some rice to go with it.

While my meal cooked, I returned to the cup I'd abandoned on the table. The locket would not defeat me. Besides, I could feel my mother judging me from the grave for having gave up on it. When I picked it up, I expected to feel the weight of the metal and even hear the chain rattling inside, but the cup was light and when I stuck my finger into the cool liquid; I found nothing but the bits of grime I cleaned from the jewelry before I gave up on it.

I didn't remember dropping the damn thing but still ended up on my knees searching for it. It wasn't long before I gave up my effort, completely frustrated with having lost it. My apartment wasn't that big, and there were only so many places it could be.

As I ate my dinner, I tried not to obsess over the fact that I'd lost the damn thing. I knew I had it in my possession; I was not crazy. Maybe it just wasn't meant for me to keep. I believed in the oddities of life; the unexplained occurrences that make life interesting.

After watching a bit of television, I prepped my lunch for the next day, did my nightly stretches, and hopped into bed. As I drifted off into what I expected to be another dreamless slumber, because I hadn't had a single dream in many years, I could do nothing but think about the locket.

MIND GAMES

I woke up with a terrible headache. The temperature had risen to an uncomfortable extreme, and as I pulled myself from the bed, the sweat soaked sheet resisted the pull from my skin. My disgust with my sweaty body took a backseat to the pounding in my head.

Inside my nightstand, as always, was a bottle of Aleve, the only pain medicine that didn't make me absolutely sick. Unfortunately, as I shook the bottle, I found it to be empty. I cursed my past self, who promised me she'd get more when she took the last two.

My resource became my shower. Yoga, which would have been my go-to to relieve the tension, was out of the option because it was too damn hot to be doing downward dog. Not to mention I lost my yoga mat while running from a demon dog after visiting my friend's studio.

It was so hot that even the floors were sticky. The suctioning sound as my foot lifted from the floor took me back to being a teenager hanging at the movie theater. Tuesdays meant five-dollar showings and hundreds of teenagers with spilled goods from the concession stand. I was glad I wasn't the one who had to clean up that mess.

I stripped off my clothes as soon as I made it into the bathroom, stepped into the shower and turned the squeaky handle. The water set to the coldest temperature; I braced myself for the frosty but relaxing stream, yet it never came.

Even after jiggling the handle. Nothing. I groaned and smacked the shower wall because on top of being disgustingly uncomfortable and dealing with a borderline migraine, I would now have to deal with annoyance of the Super. He was an average overweight, overpaid, bum of a guy.

Naked, I stumped back to my bed to pick up my cell phone from the nightstand and gave an angry side eye to the empty bottle of Aleve. I found his contact, captured with a picture of a dog's ass, and dialed the number. Nothing. No service. It wasn't unlike my cell service to drop, considering there were very few cell towers in the low-income area.

Determined to get this resolved, I redressed and headed for the stairs that would take me from my seventh-floor unit down to his basement hideout. I was ready to tell him to get off his ass and get my shit fixed, but found a sign posted on his door.

"We are currently experiencing plumbing issues for all tenants. This is a citywide problem. Unfortunately, there is nothing I can do for you. The city will have this issue handled as soon as they can. If you have any further questions, call the number below."

Annoyed that I couldn't voice my frustration, I hiked back up the stairs. By the time I got back to my apartment, the sweat was pouring from my pores in buckets. I stripped down to my underwear, too hot for even shorts, turned the box fan on high and pointed it directly at the bed. It was a struggle to block out the assaulting heat, but I managed and eventually returned to my fitful sleep.

FROZEN

W aking up to the chill that skittered across my skin was a mind fuck. There was no way my box fan had chilled the air that much, but still I reached to turn it off. Waving my hand like a drunk elephant, I search for the off switch but realized there was no push of air to enforce the chill that reached my bones.

My eyes opened to the visible breath that parted from my lips and I sat up to find myself on the derelict platform, the last stop on the line. The conductor's voice call out echoed in around me. The bench creaked with the shift of my weight as I searched for the man but found no one.

This had to be a dream, the first I'd had in a long time. Sudden panic caused me to look down. Fully dressed, well at least I avoided that clichéd embarrassment.

Not only was I fully dressed but hanging around my neck was the locket. Crescent shaped and perfectly polished. I studied the thing in my hand and wondered if I hadn't dreamed it up to begin with. If it were just a figment of my imagination, why did it keep coming back to me?

I left the bench, mind struggling to come up with solid explanations for my mental state. There was no doubt in my mind that I was dreaming. The nagging feeling in the pit of my stomach was the warning that things were about to get weird. I needed to wake the hell up.

"Hello." I damn near fell on my ass from fright after the voice sounded off behind me. Maybe I should have turned to investigate the source. I didn't; I made a mad dash for the exit of the platform. Whoever was lurking in the shadows could remain there, without me.

My skin was threatening to crawl right off of my body as memories of the man who died there returned to me. That feeling in my stomach only grew more intense as my legs struggled to carry me forward. But I kept running until the burn of muscle fatigue wrapped around my legs. My body crashed, and I dropped to the ground.

Despite the chill in the air, the sweat still poured from my face. Each drop instantly turned to ice in the freezing air, creating ice sickles that stuck to my skin. I fought to catch my breath as I picked the ice from my skin but froze with the sound of struggling electric pulses of a light that refused to go out. I realized it then that the ground underneath my bare legs wasn't the asphalt it should have been. No, pressed against my ass was the same rotted planks of the terminal at the last stop on the line.

"Hello." When the voice came again, I considered running, but my legs refused. Without the ability to flee, I processed the sound. A man, and from the tone of his voice he was likely mid to late twenties. Perfect, the same demographic of a dead Edward. Just what I needed in my life, to be seeing ghosts.

"You have got to be kidding me." I sighed and turned around to find the man standing just beneath the light. He was just as I remembered him from the picture. His fingers dug into the bench tight enough to leave their impressions. It was as if the bench was an anchor he was holding onto for dear life.

The man who appeared to me was tall with dark brown skin. His face bore strong features like the jawline of a proud and hardworking man. His eyes were large sad light brown orbs wrapped inside the heavy lids. He appeared timid yet anxious, as if he was waiting for something to happen. His fingers of his free hand fiddled with the buttons on his suit jacket while he chewed on his bottom lip.

I was looking at a dead man. The longer I stared, the more

resemblance I saw between the man in front of me and the one in the pictures. A businessman, I think it said something about him being a lawyer. I tried but couldn't remember the old article my mother kept, or her reasoning for keeping it tucked away inside one of her old jewelry boxes.

"Please don't run." He spoke with pleading eyes that filled me with unnecessary guilt.

"No worries there, like it did me any good the first time." I pulled myself up from the ground but kept my distance from him.

For a moment it looked as if he might grin. The corners of his mouth twitched, moving slightly upward before being pulled back into the somber expression. Maybe ghost weren't allowed to smile. It added to their ability to creep you the hell out. I wondered briefly if there was a penalty for it. Would some great ghost lord appear and drag him off to be punished if he broke the rule?

"I like you. I see you a lot. I know I wasn't supposed to, but I had to, I couldn't help it." He dropped his eyes and fiddled with the wood of the bench.

"Okay, I hate to break it to you, but you are missing some vital details in that little confession." Despite my growing panic, I remained calm. Maybe if I didn't spook the spook, I could avoid requiring an exorcism later on.

"I did it, broke your purse, your mom's purse, so you would see it, so you could see me." He avoided eye contact as if he thought I would scold him for his actions. He wasn't too far off base.

"So, you are Edward Hill?" I swallowed the knot that formed in my throat because I knew knowing his answer would be an affirmative one.

It wasn't an answer I wanted to hear. I didn't want to know that there was life after death, and that ghost and who knows what else roamed the earth and haunted those of us who were living. Or were we living? Were we all just apparitions waiting to realize the true terror of our existence? If he confirmed my thoughts, and I knew he would, it would crush my hopes for a peaceful nothingness after death.

"Yes." He raised his head, excited about my recognition. He was proud that I knew him, elated to not have gone forgotten.

"But you're dead, like gone." I paused to fact check my memory for the hundredth time. "Or at least you're supposed to be. Right, isn't that how it's supposed to work?"

"Dead, yes, gone, no, not at all. I am here, always here." He spoke in a halting pace, his words almost struggling to form. "It was terrible being here all the time, waiting. I am not sure what I was waiting for. Nothing ever changed. That is… nothing ever changed until you came. Twice a day I got to see you. Almost every day and on those days, you were always the last person I saw. I got excited when I saw you, I waited for you." He smiled a bit, and the expression was worse than the somber mask he wore before. His smile was so empty that it made my heart ache.

"Yeah, that's not creepy at all." I rubbed my arms where Goosebumps were forming. I had a dead guy as a secret admirer. There were no restraining orders against something like that. Hell, I wouldn't want to be the one attempting to explain the logistics of it. Maybe it was time I decided on an alternative route to take to work. Crazies and crack heads didn't sound too bad after all.

"Sorry." His disappointment was palpable. Did he expect a better response from the woman just told a ghost had spent months, maybe longer, stalking her?

"What's the point of all this? You wanted a friend, so you pull me into, well into whatever the hell this is?" I looked out, trying to see something beyond the darkness. All I could see is more of the thick black blanket of night that existed outside of the platform.

"You have always had the gift of sight; I only opened your eyes." He defended his actions. Just like a man to not want to accept the blame for his actions, even though he just confessed to doing it.

"Are you seriously going to be that ghost from every creepy ass horror story that speaks in riddles and annoys the hell out of me?" I tap my foot, demanding more answers. "Just say what you mean to say. I'm not one for riddles or trying to figure out what is going on inside of your

14

ghostly dome."

"Come." He held out his hand to me. I of course was in no hurry to grab hold of the creepy dead stalker guy's hand. "Please." He was nearly pouting, pathetic. And for whatever reason, I felt sorry for the guy.

"Well, since you asked nicely, and if my assumption is correct, there is no other way off this platform…" he nodded, confirming my fear. I sighed, grabbed his hand and braced for the unknown.

GONE

We were everywhere and nowhere all at the same time. Images of different blocks of time flashed before me. I witnessed girls playing jump rope, old men chewing tobacco, women and children living in huts, cowboys heading off for war, cities being built from the ground up. And then it just stopped. Everything came to a complete halt, as if time ceased to exist.

I held my hands to the sides of my head for a moment, to convince the spinning to stop. When the dizzying effect faded, and I opened my eyes, the destination left me both impressed and confused.

"A courthouse? You brought me to a courthouse?" The tall building climbed up into the void above us and appeared to never end. Tall pillars supported the balcony that sat above its doors. It looked like a mouth, like most court houses. One that sat open, waiting to chew you up and spit you out.

"Yes. This is where we all go, at some point. I suppose. For judgement." He smiled at the irony of his statement. I returned the expression for a moment before the weight of his words crushed the humor out of me.

"Wait. Hold up. You mean judged, as in judgment day, as in MY judgment day?" Of course, panic engulfed me. Who wouldn't panic at such a thought? I was only twenty-five years old. My life was just beginning! What did I do to deserve to be snatched from my world and sent to the big house?

"Yes, as in judgment day, but no, not yours. There is however something that you must do here, now that you see." He walked away from me and headed up the steps to the building surrounded by nothing. A blank slate protrudes out in all directions. I had the itch to run, but the common sense to know I would get nowhere. Hell, I *was* nowhere. Right smack in the middle of it.

"Yeah, right, now that I see." I groan. It wasn't like I asked to see anything. No one gave me the choice to decline the unwanted offer.

If they had given me a permission slip for this little field trip, I would have shredded it. Ignorance was bliss after all. Some things weren't meant to be perceived, like dead guys and courthouses where the dead go for their last judgment.

I followed Edward reluctantly into the building. With each step, I reminded myself of what he said. I was not there to be judged. The words became my mantra. If not for them, I wouldn't have been able to keep my feet moving forward.

Each step was echoed with the internal chant. I didn't want to be there at all. What I wanted is my hot apartment, barely working fan, and my fabulous new job. Apparently, what I wanted no longer mattered. I had sight, whatever the hell that was. I could see, and that's what mattered. At least that's what the ghost who led me through the courthouse said. What he hadn't told me was what the hell it meant to have this sight.

The large halls were empty but lined with odd-shaped windows. My attempts to look through them prove futile. The only thing I saw on the other side was darkness. Maybe everyone else was judged, sentenced, and sent on their way. Great, how very encouraging that was.

"Look Edward, this is fun and all, but I don't want this, I want to go home." No matter how many times I repeated the contrary to myself, I still felt like I was walking into D-Day. This was all just a terrible dream that refused to release me. No matter what ways I tried to trick my mind into returning to the conscious realm, I remained in the dream.

"That is not possible now." He kept walking ahead of me without even turning around to acknowledge my concerns. Were all ghosts as lacking in the manners department as he was? Did death take away human decency?

"And do you mind telling me why the hell not?" I demanded, no longer concerned with how aggravated the ghost would result. What the hell gave him the right to knock my life off its rails? I deserved an explanation.

"Because you, well, you're needed here, Josephine." Once again, he spoke in the puzzled language, leaving me with more questions than I had before I asked.

"How and why am I needed? I take pictures for a living. Any otherworld hoodoo is not really something I can help you out with." I stopped walking and finally he altered his course to address me.

"It's you. You have sight, you can see." Though he stopped walking, he kept his back to me. For a moment, I considered smacking him in the back of the head. I would have if I weren't so afraid of the idea of touching him. The skin on my hand still crawled, though I couldn't actually remember what it felt like to have his ghostly flesh against my own.

He started on his path again, and because I had no other option, other than remaining inside the empty hall with its odd empty windows, I followed him. I was also afraid that if I let him out of my site, one of those empty windows would open up and something would pull me inside.

Reaching the end of the hall, he pushed open the largest set of double doors I had ever seen without so much as a struggle. Just a flick of his wrist and they slid to part ways and allow him entrance. I followed him inside, because as I said before, where else was I going to go?

The doors opened to a massive courtroom filled with never ending rows of empty benches. The aisles that reached down the center stretched so far away; I gave up on straining my eyes to see the end. He started down the aisle. I bit my tongue and stopped myself from requesting a pit stop. He wouldn't listen anyway, and something told me

18

I wouldn't be able to escape the dream until I saw it through to the end.

The walk to the front of the room was surprisingly short. As if each step carried us forward twenty. Before long, we were standing in front of a podium so high that I had to crane my neck to see the top, and even then, I couldn't see the face of the person who sat behind it.

The only thing I could see was hair, no face, just the very top of an onyx-colored forehead and a blazing red afro that shot out in random areas. It was one of those carefree styles, as in 'I don't care to carry a comb', completely comical.

"Josephine Massey?" The voice boomed, nearly too loud, and it snuffed out all airs of humor that the hair produced. Did they really need to yell? It was just like that damn conductor, no one else was there. What was the point?

I kept my snarky thoughts to myself. Who knew what this ball of hair was capable of? In no way was I eager to find out that Red Fro could breathe fire.

"Yes," I respond simply.

HOME

O nce we were outside the courthouse, the world dissolved into darkness. The further we descended the stairs, the darker it got until I could see nothing, but I felt Edward's presence there for a moment longer and then even that was no longer there. I closed my eyes, hoping that I hadn't lost my sight. When I opened them again, I was home, in my hot apartment with the struggling fan.

I was almost able to convince myself it was a dream until I felt the weight of the locket around my neck. The cold metal pressed against my warm skin and brought a sense of deep concern that turned into a knot in my stomach.

I sat up on the edge of the bed and lifted the locket into my hand to examine it. Though I'd failed in cleaning it, it was spotless. I hadn't realized before because of the grime that cover it, but the locket was silver with rose gold accents. My mind shifted from the mysterious piece of jewelry to the events I still wasn't sure wasn't a dream, and I rushed to pick up the hand mirror from my nightstand.

I held the glass away from me and said a small prayer that I wouldn't find the trauma still stained on my face. Slowly, I rotated the handle, allowing it to present my reflection and my entire world eased. There were no bloodstains on my skin, no changes in my eyes or flesh. I was still me.

The deep sigh turned into a startled gasp with the sudden vibrations of my phone. I lifted my pillow to reveal the device that screamed at me. Checking the screen, I had ten missed calls and far too many unread text messages. The last four calls were from my new boss. *Great.*

My instinct was to come up with some excuse, anything that could justify my missing so many efforts to contact me. The heatwave and lack of functional plumbing were a perfect reason for the missed calls. As I swipe across the screen, I notice it was more than just the calls. She'd emailed me four times.

It took me another ten minutes to work up the nerve to return an email. That was easier, right? Before I could type the first words of my sorry apology, the phone rang again.

"Hello?" I answer the phone and tried not to sound like I had just been sleeping. Maybe if I added more urgency to my tone, she would be more concerned than upset.

"Oh, thank God! You are alright!" Her voice was a shrill mixture of worry and relief. If there were any traces of sleep left, her response to my voice had erased them.

"Yes, why wouldn't I be? I apologize for missing…" I began my explanation, but she rushed to interrupt my apology.

"Honey, it's of no concern, I'm just happy you are okay. We tried to check in with everyone after the explosion, but we hadn't heard from you."

"Explosion?" All I knew about was the dying heat, broken plumbing, and the strangest dream of my life. I would continue to refer to it as a dream until I could come up with a saner explanation for what I had just experienced.

"Yes, I can't believe you don't know, turn on the news," she instructed me. "It was so close to your address. I swear I felt the blast all the way up north!"

After struggling to reach the remote to the television, I got the screen to light up. It wasn't even necessary to change the channel. It was

21

breaking news on a channel that didn't have a news segment. There was an explosion three hours ago. I checked the screen on my phone to find that it was 11:00 p.m. I slept all day, or I was away the whole day.

"What the hell happened?" I asked her and forgot all professional demeanor as I watched the information that flashed across the screen. It provided no clarification, only jumbles of images of people and burned houses.

"They say it was a generator. Can you believe that? What kind of generator can take out a ten-block radius? I highly doubt that! I say the government is behind this, but hell, what can you do?" My new boss was a wonderful woman but also a total activist. She loved nature and mostly hated anyone who had any affiliation with the government, except of course those that claim to be on our side. Politics, right?

"This is insane!" A massive hole that was being depicted in images across the screen made me sick to my stomach. How could I have possibly slept through all of that? My boss was right, this wasn't far from my home.

"Yeah, it's so close to you! I didn't know if you would be in the area, maybe out running errands or taking photos." She rambled on, expressing the countless ways she imagined me being taken out in the blast. My mind was so consumed by my own thoughts, I let her finish hers.

It was also hard not to make a note of her exaggerations. There was no way she felt the blast from twenty miles away when the events were just a few miles from my home, but it hadn't broken the glass in my shady little window. It was going to be interesting working for her.

"Yeah, no, luckily, I was at home, because of some plumbing issues." My curiosity carried me to the window, though I knew I wouldn't see much from where I was, but I couldn't look at the screen anymore. I had to move; the images had me eager to see more.

I couldn't see anything but the lights of the emergency vehicles. How did I sleep through this? According to the woman who spoke from a studio newsroom, firefighters were still working to calm the remaining flames. Police and paramedics were scrambling to move everyone away from the affected area.

"Can I please call you back?" I ask her as I watched the flickering lights.

"Yes, sure, I am just glad to know that you were not harmed." She instructed me to take the next few days off, even though the events hadn't directly affected me.

We ended the call, but I remained by the window a moment longer, waiting, watching, and anticipating a change in the scenery that doesn't come. What I did see were a few more bodies that drifted through the streets as they were ushered further from the center of the blast. Lost faces, all shocked by what they'd experienced.

There would be no actual form of a solution or a resolution to the desolation. According to the woman on the news, whose eyes grew sadder with each passing moment, they didn't expect there to be any understanding of the cause any time soon. The area would be a madhouse for weeks, months, possibly longer.

Her job would be to squash the already rising speculations about what really caused the devastation. As her voice faded into the background, taking on that typical reporter tone, my mind grew more curious. Standing there and waiting for whatever information they approved her to regurgitate wasn't going to do it for me. I tossed on a pair of shorts and a t-shirt, stuffed my feet into my sneakers, grabbed my camera and headed out the door.

~

They crowded the streets. The dark pavement overflowed with the people who moved just far enough away to feel safe, but not so far that they wouldn't be able to still catch glimpses of the action. I pushed by them and headed for the core, taking pictures as I move.

Captured by my lens were the faces of women and children, worried and huddled together, waiting for their families or some fleeting sense of security. There were some who were badly injured, some near death. I lifted my camera to take a photo of a man with a particularly ghastly wound on his neck. What looked like a piece of metal stood from his shoulder.

23

He looked me dead in the eye as I snapped the photo, and I felt his sorrow through the viewfinder. Convinced I'd capture all of his agonies on film, I checked the display to review the image. It would be one to be recorded for history. I nearly dropped my camera after what I saw, or what I didn't see.

I lifted my eyes back to the street to be sure that the man I saw was there. He was. Standing there with his horrible injury, he continued to look at me. Again, I looked at the display to review the image and though there were people, all hurting and impacted by the moment, he wasn't one of them. This time when I looked back up, he was gone.

I swallowed back the bile as the realization settled. He wasn't there, or he was just not physically. Everything I hoped was a dream was reality. I turn from the scene of the missing man only to find myself face to face with another. He is the size of a wall, dressed in work gear and standing next to his own limp body. Blood pools from his ears as he lingered there, holding on to what was already taken from him. It's real.

As I moved further, I noticed more of these lost souls. The closer I got to the heart of the trauma, the more I witnessed. There were hundreds of them. They remained next to their loved ones and watched them for a while before accepting their fates, and moments later faded away. Some cried out, howled, and begged their families to see them, to know that they were there, but eventually, they all fade away. Then there were others who roam aimlessly, lost and unaware that their life has ended. They called for help, asking for someone to aid them, only no one did. No one could.

My focus couldn't be given to those lost souls. I had a job to do. Instead of contemplating the meaning of life, I thought about my feet moving, and my camera working to capture these terrible moments. Life was still happening all around me and dammit if I wasn't going to get the best of the worst of it.

I made it to the barricade the police created to keep everyone out while they tried to make sense of the mess. It was when I made it to the front of the line after pushing past the crowded bodies that I witnessed the image that would haunt me for years to come.

There were so many of them, hundreds of souls, standing,

waiting, lost. They all looked at me knowingly. They saw me, and they knew that I could see them, even if no one else could. Their faces, the pain of their souls, the sadness in their eyes, all impressed upon me before they vanished. It was as if passing their torture on to me allowed them freedom from this world.

I moved as close as they would allow and took pictures. Not two minutes after I started capturing images, a hand appeared in front of my lens. The images of another body being carried away on a stretcher were ruined.

"Sorry, no photography, you have to take that somewhere else, Honey." A dumpy little woman stood in front of me. The badge on her chest indicated she was CPD, and because I'd forgotten my press badge, I had no choice but to comply. I would walk into the fire, but not if it got me arrested. I couldn't imagine I would look well behind bars, and a jumpsuit in either jailhouse stripes or that Crayola shade of orange just wouldn't work for me.

Because I enjoyed freedom, I complied and moved away from her and the scene, content to take any photos I could get on my way out. Because I couldn't get the images I wanted, and the lost souls were starting to pay too much attention to me, I decided it would be best to head home.

There was a small path that would lead to the alleyways. I'd be able to move through the streets, out of the crowds that way. Before I made it to the turnoff, a small child, a boy with wide eyes and curly hair stepped in my path. He looked up to me and without hesitation grabbed hold of me. His arms wrapped around my waist and he sobbed.

"Please help me. Can you help me?" His tears caused streaks in his dirt covered skin. The boy looked as if he'd rolled around in the ashes caused by the fires.

I examined his face and found there was a little blood at the hairline above his forehead. He was clearly hurt, but it didn't seem too bad.

"I will try. Where are your parents?" I knelt down in front of him.

"I don't know, they left me, they were there, and then they were gone and I'm all alone now." He spoke his words in between small sobs and hiccups.

"What is your name?"

"Matthew." He coughed out his name and gave me a timid smile. My heart broke for the boy. He was hurt, lost, and away from his family. Going through such traumatic events was bad enough, but to be alone in it at such a young age couldn't have been easy.

"Okay, Matthew, well don't worry, I will help you find your mom and dad."

I reached out my hand to the young boy who grabbed hold. When our hands connected, there was a flash of light so bright that my eyes hurt. When my vision readjusted, I was still holding the little boy's hand, but we were no longer in the middle of the wreckage. We were standing at the steps of the courthouse.

"Where are we?" The boy looked at me with large and questioning eyes. I would have expected him to be terrified by the change in scenery, but he wasn't. Though he was concerned, he was calm.

"We are nowhere we need to be. We have to go." I tugged on his little hand and urged him to follow me.

I didn't make it two steps before the ghostly tour guide was blocking my path. I thought about trying to get around him but realized that it would be pointless. I had no idea how to get away from the courthouse.

"What the hell is this? Why are we here?" I pulled Matthew closer to me because I didn't want anything to happen to him. I felt the strongest urge to protect the little boy. He was too young to be concerned with self-preservation. He needed someone more concerned about the mysteries of life to care about what happened to him.

"Because you are a shepherd. He lost his way. You guided him to where he needed to be." Edward puffed his chest out with pride. The happy smirk, the product of his joy that I had fulfilled my duty. If he could have, he likely would have scheduled a parade for me. Though I

26

imagined the only attendees would have been lifeless and I'd had enough ghosts for one day.

"No! No, I am no shepherd! I have to get this boy back to his parents!" My outburst wiped away Edward's short display of pride.

"Yes, I know." He looked at me with understanding. The hurt in his eyes almost enough to convince me to forgive him. "But he is no longer alive, neither are his parents, this is where he is supposed to be now, Josephine."

"I don't care what you say, Edward. I am not taking him in there! He doesn't belong there!" I pushed by him and pulled Matthew with me.

"Where are you going?" Edward followed my fitful exit.

"Away from here!" I yelled at him.

"You can't do that, Josephine." He sounded frustrated, upset at my unwillingness to participate in his little game.

"Try and stop me." I challenged him without turning to face him. Why should I? It wasn't like he ever paid me the same courtesy.

"I don't have to, you can't leave here with him, it is impossible."

"What do you mean?" I turned around.

"He can't leave here. Once a spirit enters this realm, they are here, forever."

"That's not true. Don't lie to me, Edward! What about you? You leave this place all the time! You spend most of your time on that stupid rundown platform. That's how you got to me!" My temper rose as I addressed him. As much as I wanted to believe he was lying to me, my gut told me he was being honest. If nothing else, Edward was a truthful ghost.

"It's different, I don't know why, but it is. But what I know is that he cannot leave, and the longer you hold on to him, the longer you only delay what is inevitable. He will stay here, and so will you, unless you deliver him." His voice changed with that last statement from pleading to a warning. The powers at be would force me to stay if I didn't do my job. A job I never signed up for.

"This is so twisted! You want me to hand him over to that awful ticket line. What happens to him when I do? Where does he go? I can't do this, I can't be like you, Edward. I can't just accept the things that I have no explanation for!" I clutched Matthew closer to my side.

"Josephine, be reasonable about this." Edward took a tentative step towards me. He used caution as if he felt I would attack him. I honestly couldn't blame him.

"What is it that I have to be reasonable about?"

"You know what I am talking about. Accept what this is and let it go." He spoke softly and stepped to the side.

"Mom, Dad?" Matthew spoke and pulled away from me.

I saw them over Edward's shoulder. They looked like Matthew, covered in soot, scared and confused. But his mother's eyes lit up when she saw him.

My heart melted because her expression reminded me of my own mother. It's the same way she looked at me the night I came home at three o'clock in the morning. She was worried that something bad had happened to me. The reaction you would expect from any parent of a teenager who was usually in bed by eleven o'clock. She pulled me into her arms and sobbed as she thanked God for my safe return home. This was right before she cursed me out for an hour and then grounded me.

I let go of Matthew and he ran to them. They lifted him from the ground and wrapped their arms around him. His mother kissed him furiously and his father cried. Matthew smiled brightly. He touched their faces, and the image of the family united broke my heart all over again. They were reunited, a family together, and yet it was hard to see it as a happy moment because they were dead. They wouldn't return to their happy home or to their normal lives. They would stand in a line, hand in a ticket marked with an unknown destination, and then they would cease to exist.

At that moment a colossal figure, cloaked in gray and towering above the family, appeared. An arm lifted and handed the family an envelope. The father took it and opened it. He removed two pieces of paper, gave one to the mother, and kept one for himself.

He kissed them both and spoke with aggressive tears that smeared the soot on his face, "Goodbye, my loves."

He turned and disappeared beyond the doors of the courthouse.

The mother cried as she carried her son inside. He looked confused and asked about his father. She simply shook her head and sobbed. I darted up the stairs and made it through the doors in time to see the father disappear at the gray ticket window while Matthew and his mother stepped into the line at the gold ticket window.

I turned away from the scene and slammed into Edward's arms.

"This isn't right." I sobbed into his chest. "Why would you have me bring him here? Why would you have me put them back together only to rip them apart? What was the point?" I pummeled him with questions he couldn't provide the answers to. He wasn't the one doing this; it was not him who had made this my life. But he was *my* shepherd. He brought me into this world when all I wanted to do was take pictures of the one I already existed in.

Moments later, I realized that I had my face buried in the chest of a ghost. I hopped backward and shook off the feeling of crawling skin. Though I didn't mean to upset him, my apparent disgust of touching him was enough to do the trick.

"I'm sorry." He apologized and stepped further away from me.

"No, it's not you. I'm sorry. I can't take this, Edward, I can't do this. I know it's what you want and what you think I am meant to do, but I just can't."

"I understand." He sighed. I waited for him to say more, but there was nothing. He gave up on me at that moment. I was relieved, yes, but also sad, disappointed that I couldn't be what he wanted and that I couldn't face his world.

RETURNED

The darkness swallowed me again, and when it released me, I was back at home. I should have found the same relief I did before, but suddenly my apartment seemed smaller, unimportant. It was still my own, but it hardly mattered anymore.

I climbed into my bed and remained there for three days. I told my new boss the things I saw at the site were too tragic and requested to have some more time to recover from the ordeal. This wasn't a complete lie.

She was sympathetic and extended my time off to two weeks. I thanked her during our call, via email, and once again via voicemail after the flowers arrived. She sent an enormous bouquet that I was grateful to have. They sat in the window seal and spread their sweet fragrance throughout the tiny apartment.

After the third day of wallowing, I got up. I walked to my window, the one that barely opened, and I saw the remaining devastation. The authorities were still working to clean up the mess. The skeletons of places that were once called home were being torn down as they would soon prepare to rebuild the neighborhood.

The city had already evacuated everyone from the affected areas. The bodies that were found had been carted away, though more names appeared on the news each night. The body count rose, fifty-six lives lost. That was the total the last time I checked, fifty-six lives taken, fifty-six souls to go to the courthouse to face their judgment. I wouldn't be their shepherd, their leader to the other side.

"Josephine?" I heard Edward's voice from behind me. It was soft, caring, and slightly afraid. This was the fourth time he visited me. The first three times I yelled at him, blamed him for what was happening, and told him to go away. Each time he left without another word.

"You're back again." I pressed my forehead against the cool glass of the window.

"Yes, sorry." He stepped closer, and the coolness that followed him touched the back of my neck.

"Don't be. I have decided not to blame you." I left the window, stepping around the intruder to return to my bed.

"Really? Why?" He followed me, pleased by my change of heart.

"Well, I have the gift of sight. I was born with it, right? While I realize that you may have helped to unlock it, I understand now that it was always there. And I have a feeling it would have happened with or without your interference." Lying in bed for days, all I had to fill the time were my own thoughts. What I took away from that was a feeling of certainty. This was all going to happen with or without Edward, and with or without my cooperation. My mother believed in destiny, and though sometimes I tried to deny it, I believed in it too.

"Yes, possibly." He didn't mean to cause me pain or to put me in the position I was in. He just wanted me to be able to see him. He wanted to not be alone anymore. I couldn't blame him for that. Edward was all alone for years. If in his shoes, I would have done anything to end that sentencing.

For the first time, I really looked at Edward, because he was there in front of me and I was tired of staring at the walls. He was tall, handsome with broad shoulders that tilted slightly to the left and a deep tawny complexion paired with light brown eyes.

His eyes were both welcoming and sad, as if he carried all the woes of the entire world with him. Even as he smiled, those eyes revealed the truth. He was alone, afraid, unhappy.

I pat the bed beside me, and after a moment of hesitation, he joined me. We didn't speak because there was nothing to say. We watched television, laughed a few times, and even glanced at each other from the corners of our eyes.

I made a pizza, which I ate alone. He watched, and I caught him licking his lips once or twice. After my third slice, he tells me that he often wished he could eat. He still had the sense of smell and it was something like torture for him not to be able to enjoy life's delicacies. I apologized and scoffed down my food quickly as not to prolong his punishment.

The next four days were enjoyable. Edward told me about his life. If he hadn't died, he would have been forty-one, sixteen years older than I was. He didn't know what happened to him, or the reason behind his death. He remembered leaving home, kissing his fiancé goodbye as he headed off to work. He made it to the train twenty minutes early and settled in on his bench with the morning paper as he waited.

He was trying to find the times and showings for the Drive-In for date night with his future wife. The next thing he knew he was watching himself being carted away on a stretcher. The paramedics had tried and failed to revive him. They looked confused, and the woman whose name tag read T. Darling said that she saw nothing wrong. There were no signs of trauma, either external or internal. They would have to test more at the hospital. Edward tried to go with them, but when he lifted his hand from the bench, something pulled him away from the physical world.

He spent a long time on the steps of the courthouse after refusing to get in line. He thought that something would change, hoped that he would wake up, but of course that didn't happen. It was her voice, the voice of his fiancé that pulled him back into the land of the living. Every night for nearly a year, his fiancé, Delilah came to that bench. She sat and sobbed for him, and he was there each night right by her side.

When she left, she would drop a rose petal. It was their thing. When they first started dating, Edward couldn't offer her flowers. He couldn't afford the bouquets that lined the windows of the local flower shop. So, each night, he would give the owner of that shop a nickel for a hand full of petals and he would bring them to Delilah. She placed the petals in between the pages of her favorite book. She brought that book with her each night to visit him. Each night she read a page, and each night she left a petal. When there were no more petals, she stopped coming. But Edward still lingered with his folded ticket in his jacket pocket as time lost meaning for him.

"Until you came along, I'd been contemplating giving up. I realized that I wasn't waiting for her anymore. She'd moved on with her life. I can't tell you how many times I almost walked into that courthouse to get in line.

"But one day you came running across the platform yelling for the conductor. You missed that train. You sat on the bench, my bench and you were cursing up a storm about missing your appointment. I laughed, because I hadn't heard such foul language from a woman since my grandmother, and it was like you heard me.

"You turned to me, looked right at me, well right through me. But you knew I was there. I could feel it. It was different than the others who might get a chill if I get too close. You were aware of me. So, each day I came back to see you. I awaited your departure and return as if they were my own. As if I possessed the ability to roam with you. But each time I let go of that bench, I was back at the courthouse."

"It seems you have figured that part of things out, at least the part about leaving the bench," I teased him. "You've been here for days and you haven't been pulled away."

"It's because you are here. It seems I can go where you are. I don't know why, perhaps I am connected to you, bonded somehow." He smiled at the thought. I watched him closely as his expression changed to something of adoration for me.

The way he stared at me changed the energy in the room. Our comfortable exchange turned into something awkward. No longer okay with his presence in my bedroom, sitting across from me on my bed, I thought about him leaving. The moment the thought passed through my head; his image flickered.

"What's wrong?" I asked.

"I…" he vanished before he could explain to me what was happening to him.

"Edward?" Concern replaced my desire to be away from him. I wanted my companion back. Talk about twisted. If I weren't already seeing ghosts, I would have considered seeing a therapist. The second he was gone, his staring, his adoration, no longer felt creepy or unnerving. I wondered if that was a version of Stockholm Syndrome. Again, that would have been a great thing to discuss with a therapist.

He reappeared, and I was overwhelmed with relief. I lunged forward across the empty space between us and called him by name. Arms opened, I flew to him, through him, across the bed, and onto the floor.

"Damn! That hurt!" I realize my mistake of jumping into a ghost. Edward had already explained to me he had to want to have a physical connection before I could make contact. He had to invite the connection.

His laughter echoed my groans of pain as I struggled to get up from the floor.

"And what is so funny?" I asked as I pulled myself from the floor and straightened my shirt.

"You are. You didn't want me here; you send me away and seconds later you pull me back as if you lost your best friend." He laughed again, and I joined him for a moment because it was exactly as ridiculous as it sounded. His description paints a picture of me as the confused girlfriend who bounced around on the idea of staying together or breaking up with her boyfriend. Only Edward wasn't my boyfriend, he was, well I didn't know what he was. But I definitely wasn't booed up with a ghost.

"Very amusing," I retorted sarcastically.

"Yes, it is." He laughs again as he stands from the bed and moves towards me.

"Well, now I no longer want you here." I walked by him and plopped down on my bed.

"I doubt that." His chuckle caused his shoulders to bounce in a

34

goofy manner.

"And why is that?"

"Because, Josephine, if you really wanted me to be gone, I wouldn't be here anymore." He reached across the bed and touched my leg.

"Well, aren't you the clever one?" I snipped at him because the truth of his words resonated with me.

I wanted him to be there with me. In the short time, I'd grown accustomed to his presence. I enjoyed being with him and the idea of him leaving frightened me. The feeling was irrational. I lived alone for a long time, actually enjoyed the solace. What had changed so much that I was afraid to be alone?

That's what it was, fear. The thought of never seeing Edward again terrified me. It was completely irrational, and yet it made so much sense. Outside my door was a world full of ghosts. He was the only one I knew I could trust. The only one who wanted nothing from me but my companionship. With sight being an unknown part of my world, I wasn't sure who was trustworthy anymore, even with those who were still living.

The next week was much the same. I spent the time learning more about my newfound friend. Regardless of the circumstances or the oddities of our union, Edward was a friend. He was a friend who happened to be a ghost, a factor I desperately tried to overlook.

A few times, as we sat in silence, I found myself looking at him, but more than that, I was appreciating him. He was kind, caring, understanding, patient, funny, and well… attractive. It was when that word passed through my head that I realized I was developing a crush on a damn ghost. It was time to get the hell out of the house.

I had two days before I would need to return to work, so I decided to get out and stretch my legs. My lungs would also appreciate the fresh air. The smell of smoke had finally cleared from the area since the flames of the fires were completely snuffed out.

After taking a quick shower, eating a small breakfast, and

jotting down a quick 'To Do' list. I headed out the door. I double-checked my pocket for the list about four times as I walked down the stairs. I was forgetful, I'd accepted it, and I'd embraced it as a part of what made me the wonderful person I was.

I closed the door, pulled my seatbelt on, and released a deep breath before I nearly pissed myself.

"Where are we going?" Edward popped into the passenger seat with so much excitement that I had to stop myself from punching him. Of course, my fist would have likely gone right through his face and into the window.

"*I'm* going to run some errands, alone." I snapped, it wasn't his fault, but I was agitated and confused. I wanted to be alone, I needed time to exist without him because the cool sound of his voice excited me in a way that it shouldn't. He was a ghost, and I was still alive.

I turned the key in the ignition and waited for the rumbling sounds of life. The check engine light greets me as the engine struggled to turn over. My small prayer for success was rewarded, but I made the mental note to add a trip to the mechanic to my 'To Do' list for the day. I couldn't put it off any longer.

"Oh. Okay." I understood his disappointment, and for a moment, I thought of inviting him along.

So many times, during our talks he spoke about being able to see the changes in the world. He questioned the things he saw on the television. He wanted to know which things were real and which were fake. Even though I provided him with the answers, he needed to see it for himself.

He couldn't believe all the things that had changed in the short time since his death. He hoped to return to his old neighborhood. It was where he spent his years as a child and where he planned to watch his own family grow. I told him I would take him. It only made sense that he thought this was that time.

"I'm sorry. I just need some time to breathe, clear my head." I gave him a small sympathetic smile, hoping to take the edge off the rejection. "Edward, I need to be alone."

He faded away without a word, and I started the engine. Yes, I was jerk. Yes, I was kicking myself. I was quite good at that whole mental self-abuse thing. There was a running list of things that I periodically beat myself up about. This moment would be added to the list.

The rest of my day went smoothly. I completed my grocery shopping, picked up my dry cleaning, and even made it to the nail salon. I tried the mechanic but was met with a posted sign that reported the shop was having electrical issues and would be closed until further notice. I contemplated trying another place, but the growling from my empty stomach prompted me to return home.

My own thoughts jinxed me. I'd started the internal cheering for the success of my day as I pulled into the sparkling lot behind my building. I'd been afraid to leave the house, afraid I would run into countless spirits looking for rides to the courthouse. I hadn't seen a single one. Perhaps my new life wouldn't be as inconvenienced as I thought.

I'd loaded my arms with bags because I'd be damned if I was going to take multiple trips up the seven flights of stairs. After struggling to get the trunk closed again, I celebrated my strength and headed for the door.

"Dear?" A small shaky voice called out behind me. Though my arms were already burning, I turned to the voice because she was clearly older, and my home training said I couldn't ignore her.

When I turned, I found a small old lady hobbling towards me. She was missing her right arm and half her face was melted away, revealing the skull beneath the tissue. She had a timid presence and if she weren't so obviously dead, I would have been eager to help her. Instead of moving to aid her like I knew I should, I backed up until I hit the building door. With my arms weighed down with the bags, I had no other option of escape.

"Dear? Can you help me?" She continued her approach.

I wanted to yell, scream, but I couldn't. Once again, my fears immobilized me. I knew what is happening; I understood what I was supposed to do, but my body refused to do anything. My emotions and mind took me to another world where ghosts were terrifying entities, and if I allowed her to touch me, it would most certainly mean I'd lose my life as well.

She neared me quicker; more eager because she knew that I could see her. Lord only knew how many people she had approached, only to discover that they weren't able to see her, they couldn't help her.

She'd made it a foot away from me when the sight of the blood oozing from her left eye became enough to thaw out my limbs, yet not quite enough to get them moving.

"Help." She was no longer pleading for my assistance. This was a command. I owed it to her. Her soul was trapped on earth and I had to help her break free of this world.

"I can't. I can't help you." I barely got the words out of my mouth because I was choking on my fears.

"Help!" she yelled at me and her one remaining arm reached for me.

My eyes bulged as her blood-covered hand approached my face. That was enough to finally wake my body up. But it came too late. I'd taken half a step when her cold hand clamped around the back of my neck and denied my escape.

The pain was instant and unbearable. Her fingers fastened into my neck and her nails pierced the layer of my flesh. My ears rang and blood spilled from my eyes, nose, and ears. My mind ached as the internal wall built to keep this new life out, crumbled, and turned to dust. With its destruction came a light as hot as the sun that seared the inside of my eyes.

Unable to scream because my mouth was full of blood, I hung there, suspended by her grasp until she released me. I crashed to the concrete, bruising my knees and breaking the glass jars in the bags I carried. When I looked up, the woman was gone, but her presence lingered.

I backed myself against the door, and through blood-tinted vision, scanned the parking lot. There were no signs of the old lady or anyone else. The relief set in. At least I wouldn't have to explain to my neighbors, or potentially the police, why blood spilled from every orifice of my face.

I sprinted up the stairs to my apartment, and lucky enough avoided running into any of my neighbors. All I needed was old lady Jenkins reporting me to the super as some sort of drug addict. As one of the tenants who complained the most, that man was looking for any reason at all to kick me out.

"Edward!" I called him as the apartment door slammed behind me and I dropped my bags to the ground.

He was there before I finished calling his name and he caught me just as my legs gave out. I couldn't hold myself up and I didn't want to. I wanted to forget the old woman and erase the image of her distorted face from my mind. If I could remove every event of the past two weeks of my life, I would, even if that meant losing the memory of Edward. He was the reason for it. This sweet, sad ghost had brought hell into my life.

"It's okay, Josephine, I'm here." With the tenor of his voice, the last traces of the pain in my head dulled, and I slipped into unconsciousness.

I awoke to his watchful eye. His face was a mask plastered on to hide his own concern and panic.

"What happened?" I adjusted myself from the awkward position in the bed.

"I wish I could tell you, but I don't know." He moved from the chair to the bed and laid his hand on my leg. "What happened to you?"

"Um," I touched my forehead as I recalled the moments before I called out to him. "There was a woman, a ghost. She came to me and I've never been so terrified. She touched me and it was nothing like Matthew, the little boy. This was violent, and I started bleeding the same way I did in the courthouse. There was so much pain. I'm not sure if it was her pain or mine but I couldn't take it."

Edward stood from the bed and paced the floor. He chewed on his lip and mumbled under his breath about how things weren't meant to be like this. Driven by thirst, I left the safety of the bed and within two

JESSICA CAGE

steps my right knee gave out and I went tumbling in Edward's direction.

I braced myself for impact with the hardwood because he was focused on his own thoughts and not welcoming my touch. Instead, I landed clumsily into his arms. His arms wrapped around me and his hands gripped the bared flesh of my back. I shivered a little from the contact. When the initial shock of his touch wore off, I realized the difference.

Not only should I have been on the floor, but there were no prickly feelings passing across my skin. His icy hands warmed, and he felt normal, real, alive. Even more concerning, the growing feelings, those inappropriate thoughts I had about the man who really wasn't, came rushing to the surface. He was real, which somehow meant my affection, arousal, and intrigue were free to be explored.

"I can feel you," I whispered to him.

"I noticed that." He carefully pushed away from me and locked those wide eyes on my face.

"What happened? What changed?" I asked him. "Before, when you touched me, I was aware of it, but I couldn't feel it. I couldn't really tell how it felt. It was more like being pricked with a thousand dull needles, but now you feel normal to me. Regular, almost like you are alive. How is that possible?"

"I don't know, but there is something I have to do, something I need to do before I lose the nerve or you push me away or whatever this effect is, goes away." His voice, lower and urgent, is coated with the same inner turmoil I was feeling. Only he wasn't questioning it like I was.

I knew it was coming and yet I did nothing to stop it. Edward pulled me into his arms and with less than a second of hesitation pressed his lips against mine. I didn't pull away from him. Logic told me I should have. That annoying little voice that yells at you and tells you to stop and go the other way. The little heifer was louder she'd ever been before, but I ignored her. Because it felt too good to be in his arms.

This ghost that shouldn't have even been allowed to touch me had come to mean so much to me in so little time. The one who waited for me each day and greeted me even though I hadn't known he was

40

there. He sat by my bed when I was sick; he was patient with me when I refused his company; he shared his life with me and expected nothing in return. And even though moments before, I had all but wished him away; he was the only person I wanted to be with. He was the only person, dead or alive, that really mattered. Who else could I run to with all the ghostly mayhem that was happening around me? Who else would have understood it and accepted me for it?

As I consider all the reasons I allowed his hands to roam my flesh, our kiss continued. It grew more persistent with each passing moment, and the remaining chill of his touch vanished. As my body temperature raised with my arousal, so did his.

There was nothing to stop us, and nothing that I wanted to interrupt what was happening. Edward was gentle yet strong and made me feel comfortable in ways I hadn't experienced with a man. From the way he kissed me, to the way he undressed me, his concern was my pleasure.

That night I made love to a ghost. The next morning, I woke up to a demon.

ORIGINS

A beastly thing hung over my bed, watching me with eyes that threatened to devour me. Its eyes glowed a fiery red, and it bared dagger-like teeth to me. It looked like a threatening scowl at first but turned into a sinister smile. This thing was actually happy to see me.

My fear turned into a sickening confusion as it parted its lips and spoke.

"Hello, daughter. I have been waiting for you." The gritty voice filled my mind and left physical impressions on my soul.

I screamed so loud that it felt as though the pressure released by my vocal cords would shred the inside of my throat. Edward jumped from the bed beside me, startled by my sudden outburst. He was always there, and once again I am grateful for his presence. He was a relaxing welcome home from my nightmares.

"Is it the same dream as before?" He cradled me in his arms as if he could protect me from the demons that hid inside of my own subconscious.

The vision came to me each night. The beast that claimed to be my Father was always waiting, haunting me with his demonic appearance. Each time escape from the dream left me pouring in sweat and frightened at my core. As much as I want to express everything that happened to Edward, I couldn't.

I never remembered much about it, other than opening my eyes and seeing the beast hanging its head above my own. Edward was comforting and each time he held me, he dabbed my forehead with a cool towel and rocked me until I fell to sleep again. He doesn't sleep. It's one of those things that are no longer necessary for a ghost. He did, however, join me in bed because having him near made the night terrors easier to battle through.

Despite the trauma that found me when I slept, I still had to return to normal life. And it was good, mostly. I went to work and took beautiful pictures, a few I'm sure will land me more recognition if published. The only problem I had was the people. Most of my days I tried not to speak to anyone for fear of engaging in a conversation with a ghost in front of my boss.

It happened my second day back to work. I stepped on an elevator and had a full conversation about poodles with a woman. I didn't realize she was a ghost until the next guy entered and nodded to me before standing inside her. She laughed at me, winked, and disappeared. I blamed my wide-eyed expression on a wayward contact and darted out of the elevator on the next floor, even though it wasn't mine.

I also learned to accept my calling, if that's what it was. My refusal to aid the lost souls always ended in my agony. There were only so many times I could bleed from my eyes before I actually lost my mind. Though I had a lot of self-deprecating habits, I wasn't one for self-inflicted pain.

Edward was proud of me when I gave in to the role. Instead of running from them, I offered my help, my hand, and guided each one to the courthouse. It got easier with time, letting them walk into their unknown future. The hardest ones were always the children. I never realized how many of the young died. Each time I wondered if they would forsake the soul. The only way to know for sure would have been to follow them, grab a ticket, and disappear into the void. Of course, this wasn't something I would be doing. I guess there would always be some mysteries to life.

For the first time in days, my phone rang, and it wasn't my boss.

Trust me, this was a relief because the last time she called it was to chew me out over some procedurals I forgot to complete. To be honest, I was on thin ice with work. I either had to balance my ghostly duties with my day job or I would need to look for another gig.

The caller ID showed that it was Mackie, a long-time friend, and creative supporter. I realized, as always when I saw her name flash across my phone screen, that I missed her. Mackie was the friend I needed. Never clingy and never wondered where I was. I didn't have to check in with her every day to know that we were still friends. She understood my need to hide away in my bunker to recharge my creative battery.

Yes, she was my best friend, but we barely ever talked, and we saw each other even less, but when I needed her, she was there, and she knew that she could expect nothing but the same from me. We'd gone months at a time with not so much as a text message and come back together as if it were only yesterday that we last spoke.

Mackie was a woman of strength. She had the frame of a bodybuilder; short and boxy. Her medium was metalworking and the daily practice of her craft left her with arms worth showing off. Which she did almost every day. If it weren't snowing outside, Macki would be showing off her sculpted arms. I used to envy her arms before I got my lazy ass back into the gym. I could match her bicep for bicep, and we would often compare our definition like two beefed-up men.

"Let's meet up. How soon can you squeeze me into your calendar?" She never bothered with the typical pleasantries, used to start a conversation. Mackie preferred to do all that face to face, and more often than not when we spoke on the phone it felt like a conversation held over text messages.

"Today works for me. Let's say two o'clock?" I doubled checked the clock to make sure I had enough time to meet. Four hours should be enough.

"Perfect, the usual?" Our usual spot had become the new Noodles & Co. It meant driving into the city, but I could use some nice light grub.

"Sounds good. See you then!" A smile stretched across my

face as I hung up the phone, and Edward's face mirrored my happy expression. It felt good to have some normality to look forward to.

Before I stepped foot into the restaurant, I devised what I thought was a solid cover story. If she asked about the explosion, I would just say I took photos and sold a few. Which was the truth; I made a nice little bundle off of the sale of those shots and still had more that I could sell. She already knew that I was safe. I sent out a mass email and text messages to inform anyone I thought would care. Also, to avoid being bombarded with a million calls and having to repeat the same conversation over and over.

When asked about my love life, I would report I had no romantic interest. There was no way in hell that Mackie would consider earth-shaking sex and trips to a courthouse in the sky with a ghost to be remotely in consideration of the category of romance.

Our meal at the restaurant was quick and allowed for just enough time for her to invite me to her showing the next night. She was also a painter in addition to metalworking. She proudly reported that her work would be on display at a local gallery called Mystique. She glowed from within as she told me the news. Mackie had been hoping to get Mystique to pick up her work for years.

After celebrating her success, the conversation shifted focus to mine. I realized then that I hadn't really spoken much about my achievements. Conversations with Edward lately revolved around ghosts, nightmares, and believe it or not, my check engine light. We celebrated being two young Black women really claiming our space in industries that typically didn't hear our voices.

I promised her I would be at her showing, and she promised me she would allow me to take photos of her. I wanted to pitch a write up about her to my boss to be featured in the 'Talent on the Rise' section. The feature could really boost her career and hopefully put me back in good standing. I left that bit out the conversation.

The next night, as I prepared for the event, I turned on my music and bounced around the apartment. It was all I could do to ignore the sulking man in the corner. The pout painted on Edward's face remained there because he couldn't accompany me to the event. He'd been so excited when I told him about it, but quickly I realized that was because he wanted to attend.

I tried my best to explain without hurting his feelings that I didn't want him to go. It wasn't because I didn't want to be with him or have him experience new things. It was too risky. What if I forgot myself and was seen talking to him, or more accurately put, talking to no one at all?

That would be a great impression to make on all of Mackie's artsy friends, the girl who talks to the air. I might as well make myself a part of the exhibit. Even as he pouted, he helped me with my dress zipper and then kissed the back of my neck softly before using my shoulders to turn me to face him. He planted a good heavy kiss on me and when I opened my eyes; I was standing alone with my knees shaking like leaves on a tree.

He was getting better and better at that. Before, his appearance was reliant on my desire to see him. That was no longer the case. Edward came and went as he pleased. I liked it, and yet I didn't. I mean, it took away from the whole privacy thing when a person could just pop in on you whenever the hell they felt like it.

He hadn't really taken advantage of the element of surprise. He even knocked before he entered my space. I'd be sitting and reading a book, and then the sound of knuckles against wood would echo inside my head. Most times I would nod, and he'd appear. A few times, however, when I wanted to be alone, I shook my head no, I'd feel a slight chill on my neck, and he'd leave.

Once again, my car started up with no problem. I sent a silent thank you to whoever was watching over me and still allowing me to ride on luck in my little bum of a vehicle. I drove to the city again because the train schedule was even more restrictive on the weekends. The last thing I needed was to miss the last train out and then have to pay for a fifty-dollar cab ride back home. On the way, I stopped and grabbed a snack, just in case the food was lacking at the showing. The last time I attended a gallery show I was starving and all they offered were grapes and cheese. *Fancy.*

The gallery was stunning, in that high-priced sort of way, but if you shelled out enough money, any hole in the wall could become something to awe. As I navigated the room, I remembered being a girl with my mother and attending a gallery. I was so terrified to even exist in the space because of how fragile everything looked. Should you touch anything, it would shatter, and every pair of eyes would be glued to your embarrassment. As far as I was concerned, heavy breathing was too dangerous an activity. If anything cracks under the pressure from my sigh of boredom, well, they'd be out of luck because I couldn't afford to replace a single thing.

Though I made it early, I sat outside and allowed more people to arrive and fill the space. I was too awkward to be the first one there. Besides, it would give Mackie more time to mingle with her other buds before I waltzed in. This way I could snag some of her time before the next wave of art lovers pushed me away. I had no intentions to battle it out for her extended attention.

My plan was executed perfectly. After the third group entered, I made my appearance. I had just enough time to hug Mackie and tell her how much I absolutely loved her work, and then my little butt was promptly shoved aside by a bubbly mass of a woman. She was in such a rush to get to Mackie that she pushed her way past thirty other people who all shot her evil glares. She deserved some of those death stares, as the woman had crushed some pretty expensive shoes on her way.

"Mackie, darling! Brilliant, simply brilliant!" That is all I heard before I hightailed it away from the area and went to view more of my brilliant friend's paintings and sculptures.

The event went well, and I stayed for two hours, which was just long enough to hear Mackie's speech, after which there was no reason for me to stay. Loved my girl, but her art friends were a snooze, and the "after-party" they were going on about sounded like a total coma inducer.

I smiled as I approved my car which waited for me, ticket free, on the city street. It's more of a 'Please don't conk out and leave me stranded' kind of smile. Pathetic and I know it. I hopped inside, hoping my baby would be good to me just once more. Placed the key in the ignition, turned it, and yep, you guessed it… nothing! A big old fat steaming pile of nothing. Not even the sad sounds of an engine

47

attempting to turn.

Several more attempts brought the same result and even more disappointment. The old girl had finally given up on me. Not even a glimmer of hope, there's nothing left, she was gone. Prior knowledge of the unavoidable doom was not enough to stop the curses that flew from my mouth mostly directed at me and my disregard for standard vehicle care.

Because of my neglect, I was stuck in the city, miles away from home! I pulled out my cell phone and begin scrolling through my contacts, hoping to stumble across a name of someone who was even slightly reliable and not halfway across the world. Also, someone with a car would be nice. Most of my friends lived in the city and refused to buy cars because there wasn't any parking and public transportation was readily available. If I'd moved to the city as planned years ago, my old junker would have been long gone.

An abrupt tap on the window left my heart pounding and my phone on the floor on the passenger side of the car. I twisted my neck to find a dark figure staring at me through the fogged glass. Using my sleeve to clear the window and my view, I reveal a fine specimen of a man looking back at me. The living, warm-bodied kind of man.

Yes, I know, it's weird that I have to specify that he was alive, but hell, I saw dead people all the time. Slowly, I cranked the window, *yes crank, because my baby was an old one*, and peeked at him through the cracked space.

"Yes?" I asked the stranger.

"I couldn't help but notice you have been sitting in this car for a while. Is something wrong?" He spoke with a deep voice so smooth I could feel its caress reaching beneath the layer of my dress and coaxing a more primal side of me. My eyes locked on his full lips and I licked my own.

His lips spread into a wide smile as he noticed my admiration.

"Actually, my car seems to have died." I kicked myself internally for easily offering up the information. Yes, this guy was highly attractive, but attractive people were often serial killers. For all I knew, his plan was to reach into my car and slice my throat open. He did say he'd been watching me. That was a major red flag right there.

My thoughts briefly go back to a newspaper article about this really twisted serial killer. The guy was sick, strangling girls and leaving their bodies in houses that were listed for sale. I take solace because his crazy ass was nowhere near my hometown. If he hadn't migrated and taken his show on the road.

"Well, perhaps I can help?" He stepped back a bit from the window and allowed me a full view of his body. He was tall, I estimate a few inches over six feet. His broad shoulders carried a light jacket over a thin tan shirt that laid against his body like a second skin. The tight fit of his clothing showed off the contours of the muscles in his arms, chest, abs, and of course, it led my eyes down his body to his thighs. I could go no further as the car door blocked the view, but I'd seen enough. This tall dark man with low-cut hair and a bright smile looked too good to be true.

"Unless you have a tow truck in your pocket, I don't see how." I joked lightly in a pathetic attempt to distract myself from the specimen in front of me. My thoughts had gone astray, though he wasn't completely innocent. I watched his eyes dart down to my top and back up a few times.

"No tow truck, but I do have a car. Maybe you need a jump for the battery?" He smiled and I nodded because that smile was both brilliant and enticing. "You don't even have to get out of the car if you know how to pop the trunk."

"We can try it, but I can't say that I'm all that convinced that it will work." The last jump I got barely took hold, and even then, I was given a stern warning to replace the part as soon as possible. Did I listen? *Of course not.*

"Great, I'll be right back." His retreating form allowed me a perfect view of his assets, the firm and plumped kind that hung out in the back and just begged to be held on to. I couldn't help but look, I liked a nice ass and his was very nice. It's the kind of ass that just screams, "This man does squats!" *Damn.*

I shook my head and pushed away from the thoughts yet

again. This was highly inappropriate. I didn't know this man, and I was somewhat involved. Even though my current significant other was a ghost, and well, how far could that really go? Still, it was no excuse for me to be acting like a cat in heat.

I retrieved my phone from the floor to send a text to Mackie. "If I go missing, a tall dark stranger in a Kia Soul has taken me, hopefully as his love slave." She wouldn't get the message until later because shed locked her phone away as she usually did during her events. Fingers crossed; I hope for the best.

The dark stranger attempted jumping the battery three times, but it did nothing. Tired of peeking through the small space beneath the hood, I got out of the car to watch him work as he attempted for a fourth time to save the day. This car was a goner, but hell, a passionate man working to revive the lifeless machinery was pretty damn sexy. My mind was far too busy tracing the outline of muscles in his arms to give a damn about the dead battery. He'd worked up a sweat, which left his jacket laying across the seat of his car.

"I guess it really is dead," he admitted after he lowered the hood and returns to my side of the car. I could see it was hard for him to admit defeat. Men and their machines, I would never understand them.

"Yeah, I figured as much. It's my own fault. The check engine light has been on for, well, for far too long. I've also gotten a few stern warnings about needing to get work done on it. I just never got around to doing it." I kicked the tire and leaned against the side of the car.

"Well, do you have a way to get home? I could at least offer you a lift." He smiled and once again, I did an internal back flip.

"You may decide to retract that offer when you hear that I live about an hour's drive south of here." I smiled at him and pulled out my phone to once again begin my search for a friend with wheels.

"Yes, perhaps I might, or maybe not, considering I too am not a city dweller. I stay about an hour south of here as well." He smiled again, and I wished he would stop just long enough for me to clear my head and properly consider his offer. While kind, he was still a stranger, and I was a single woman with no one who would immediately worry about me f I went missing. But it was cold, dark, and I hadn't been able to reach anyone who could help me. A taxi or Uber would have been just as risky.

"Are you sure?"

"Yes, so, Ms...." He trailed off, not knowing what to call me as I never gave him my name.

"Josephine," I offered, eager to hear my name rolling off his tongue and across those sexy lips.

"Josephine," And of course it sounded just as good as I imagined, if not better. "Would you like a lift home?"

The smart thing for me to do at that moment would have been to return to the gallery, wait out the boring party and then burden Mackie with the joy of driving me a full hour out of the way, but I didn't want to do that. This was her big night and the last thing she needed to be doing was playing chauffer to me.

I decide to take the risk. My reason being that it was just like hailing a cab or calling an Uber. I'd still be putting my life and safety into the hands of a stranger either way. "Okay, sure." Hell, I knew how to protect myself. A girl doesn't take four years of self-defense classes without picking up a thing or two about fighting off tall sexy men.

"What is your name?" I asked before opening the passenger door to grab my keys and other essential items from the inside of the car.

"Sam." He said his name in such a seductive way I would have sworn he'd practiced it for years to produce such a quality. "Sam Merrit."

"Nice name." I tossed a duffle bag at him and he caught it easily. Figured I might as well take as much as possible, considering the state of my car, the city would more than likely have it towed away. Which meant paying more than the damned thing was worth to get it back. I tapped the old girl on the hood and walked away.

"Is it?" He opened the passenger door for me and tossed my bag in the back seat after I was inside. I waited for him to make it to the driver's seat before responding and watched him through the window as he rounded the car.

51

"Yes. I like your name." It wasn't the name as much as the way he said it and the dance that began in between my legs. That part of my thought, I kept to myself.

"Well thank you, I guess."

I couldn't help the laughter when his cheeks reddened. I'd actually made him nervous with my response. My only guess was that he was used to girls falling all over him, and not a woman who would be direct with her thoughts. It didn't matter how many internal somersaults I did; I would never perform acrobatics for a man.

The longer we drove, the more I noticed how intimidated he was. As the vehicle pulled onto Lakeshore drive, there were actual beads of sweat on the man's forehead.

"Do you know where you're going?" I nearly choked on my laughter.

"What?"

"I mean, I know we both live south of the city, but you never asked my address."

"Oh, crap, I'm sorry. What is it?"

I give him my address and he laughed because he lived exactly one mile further south than I did. He even went so far as to recite his own address so I could text it to my closest friend.

"How do I know this is your real address?" I asked as I typed the details in a message to Mackie.

"You can check my ID if you'd like." He pointed to the dashboard where he'd slid his wallet after getting into the car.

"I'll take your word for it."

"I appreciate that." He winked. "So, what do you think you will do about your car?"

"I'll call for a tow in the morning. I have no idea what I will do with it after that. I wasn't planning on getting a new car right now, but maybe it's time for something new. I'm sure the best I'll be able to do is sell it to a junker." I looked out the window at what my mother said was the sexiest skyline in the world.

"It really is beautiful, isn't it?" Sam remarks. "That skyline is one of the reasons I still live here. Don't get me wrong, I'd never get a place in the city, but that view makes that hour long drive worth it."

The conversation ended there. The next twenty minutes of our drive happened in total silence. Sam periodically looked my way as I looked his. There was more than nerves there. Sam looked concerned. But about what? His hands tightly gripped the steering wheel, his teeth captured his bottom lip, and he shifted around in his seat.

"Something on your mind?" I question him because I got that tingle of intuition in my stomach, the one that told me to be cautious, but I had no Idea what it meant so foolishly, I ignore it.

"Yes," he responded and went right back to chewing on his lip.

"Okay, care to expand on that answer?" I wasn't a mind reader. If he wanted to discuss whatever was bothering him, he'd need to use words.

"Yes, I'd love to. Problem is that I'm not sure that I should." He glanced over and the eye contact makes me physically ill. My stomach twisted into knots. That intuition was telling me to run for the hills. Too bad I was in a vehicle going at least sixty miles an hour down the expressway.

"Why not?" Did I really want him to answer? Would it not be better for him to go on chewing his lip until he dropped me off at my place? He could leave me with fading thoughts of his sexy ass and arms.

"I'm not so sure that you're ready to hear what I have to say, Josephine." He kept his eyes trained on the road ahead as he spoke.

"Okay, that's a strangely deep thing for you to say to me considering we only met about an hour ago." I wanted it to sound like a joke, something to lighten the mood, but my voice betrayed me and leaked my suspicion into the car.

"Yes, I know, but it appears time is running out and minutes ticking away on a clock cease to have real meaning."

The hairs on the back of my neck stood because his words remind me of the puzzling way Edward spoke when we first met. A thought followed by a strong sense of guilt. Edward. Would he be upset with me for accepting a ride from Sam? It wasn't like he could have done anything to help me, considering his state of being.

"Okay, just spit it out. Whatever it is," I urged him to fill my mind with anything but the ghost. If I thought about him too much, he might actually appear and that was the last thing I wanted to happen.

"Your father is coming, Josephine." He does just as I asked, spits it right in my face and I am pissed! Before I could question his words, he continued speaking. "I know this sounds insane, but he knows that you have Sight now, and he wants to use you to aid him in his war. You are a shepherd of lost souls and the daughter of a demon. Which means you can guide those souls to him if you choose to."

"Pull over!" I ordered. He quickly pulled the car off to the shoulder of the road and I jumped out the second it the wheels stopped moving.

The door slammed behind me and as much as I wanted to run off into the night, I couldn't. There was nowhere for me to go. Cars sped past us and the nearest exit was still several miles away. Instead of running I looked to the sky and screamed. I pulled the anger from deep within and unleashed it on the night.

Sam stood there; eyes locked on me. I had no words to say. How could I possibly express what I felt when I didn't know what it was? I wanted to call him a liar, but that annoying feeling in my gut told me he wasn't. Besides, I was still being haunted every night by images of a demon who claimed to be my father. Each time I closed my eyes, he was there with the same message. He was waiting for me.

Sam might as well have been reading from a transcript of that dream. On top of his accurate depiction of my demonic father, he knew about Sight. He spoke about it as if it were a common topic. His truth, his admission, it tore me up inside because I had truly convinced myself that I was done with getting paranormal surprises.

I saw dead people, a gift I was apparently born with. It was my ob to usher them to the other side. Was that not enough? The universe, the fates, just had to toss in some dark ass demon daddy to spice things up. God only knew what he expected me to do for him.

My brief outburst ended and instead of returning to the car, I paced the ground and pulled my jacket tighter around me. I could feel Sam's gaze focused on my movement and from time to time, I glanced at him. My mind struggled to find the right words to say. I had so many questions, but every time I attempted to ask one, my brain lost all concepts of the English language.

The only thing I was sure of was that I wanted to talk to Edward. He could explain this and if not, he would have to know how to find the right information. But I couldn't call him to me. I couldn't ask him those questions in front of Sam. I didn't want to hurt Edward, he didn't deserve that.

"Who are you?" The understanding of language returned to me and my feet stopped moving.

"I'm Sam," he replied in a condescending tone, as if I had completely lost my mind.

"Not your name, I know your damn name! Tell me who you are. How do you know about Sight, about me, and about my Father?" Instead of answering my question, he chewed his lip again, buying himself more time. "Answer me!" I demanded.

"I know about you because I am like you, Josephine. I have Sight as well. I'm also a shepherd. I am here to help you, Josephine." The man was a statue leaning against the hood of the car. Those deep eyes locked on me.

"And how convenient that you were there to help me the very night my car dies?" I stomped closer to him, ready to test out my kickboxing skills. "Did you do that? Did you sabotage my car?"

"Yes, I did. I had to if I was going to get anywhere near you without that damn ghost boyfriend of yours. By the way, what you two are doing is not okay, I hope you know that." His scolding came with a tinge of jealousy. Who the hell was he? I was so sick of people, otherwise known as men, popping into my life and deciding they could just switch everything up

55

when they damn well pleased.

"That's none of your business. If I wanted your opinion, I would have asked you for it," I paced a bit more but skid to stop after considering his words. "Wait, you've been watching me? Spying on me like some sick pervert in the bushes? How the hell did you know about Edward?" I screamed at him now over the sound of cars passing us by.

"I had to. Josephine, I had orders to follow." His gaze locked with mine and told me what he couldn't say out loud.

Sam hated his job and whoever issued the orders. Maybe I should have been sympathetic to his pain. I wasn't. I didn't give the man an invitation into my life. I don't care who his boss was. He'd invaded my privacy and to top it off, destroyed my car.

"Orders from who? What the hell are you talking about?" Paranoia had me looking out into the surrounding darkness, fist poised for attack or defense.

"Look, we can stand here and argue, and you can fight the imaginary people, or we can get back in the car and I can answer whatever questions you have for me. It's obvious that you are lacking the information you need. I'm surprised they haven't reached you by now." He moved to open the passenger door for me to return to my seat inside. "It's been weeks since your eyes were opened. There's a lot to discuss, Josephine. Please believe me when I say that I only intend to help you. That is all."

I stomped over to him, peering deep into his eyes and become instantly defeated. He was telling the truth. There was an odd light behind the iris of his eyes. The same one I noticed in my own. It's a slight change, so slight that no one else seemed to notice. But I could see it there, wrapped around the green and highlighting the gold flecks that dance in his eyes.

I had nothing more to say. We were the same. I climbed in the car and refastened my seatbelt as he moved to return to the driver's side.

"Tell me everything," I say before he can shift the car into gear.

TRUDENT MASSEY

"Sight is something you inherit. It's passed down from generation to generation. In your case, it was your mother. She was extremely gifted, amazing at what she did. I remember growing up and listening to the stories about her. Your mother was different. She saw more than what any other person with the gift could see. Her visions weren't limited to spirits.

"Your mother could see other worlds, worlds that no one could have ever contemplated existing. That wasn't enough for her, simply seeing them. She honed her powers and eventually she could cross the barriers between realms. Years would go by and your Trudent Massey would come back as if it had been no more than a day. People envied her for that because essentially your mother could use doors and passageways to escape time." Sam spoke from the seat beside me. The car remained still on the side of the road.

"What else do you know?" I asked simply. I had to know everything, even the hard things. Sam praising my mother wasn't going to help me figure things out.

"It's also known that your mother fell in love with a demon. In full knowledge of what he was. Her judgement was not clouded by tricks as everyone initially thought. She felt like she could change him for the better. Once she realized that she couldn't, she ran, and with her, inside

JESSICA CAGE

of her, she took a child, his daughter.

"When your mother died, it wasn't a part of a modern-day plague. It was a part of a mass assassination. All those who died were Sighted. Each name on the list was of someone who was feared to have the ability to cross through the worlds. Unfortunately, there were only a few who even came close to what your mother could do. It was a plot to eliminate the Sighted ones, which would leave souls lost, unable to cross to their rightful resting places, and vulnerable for the demons to take, to fuel their plots to cross into the other realms. This assassination was in vain. When one person with sight perishes, another is born, or more like awakened. There are millions of people who have the gift of Sight buried inside of their DNA but not all are aware of it. Most will live their lives completely uninhibited by it.

"Your mother thought that she could hide you from your father, but demons are forever connected to anything that they create, and above all else, they are connected to their offspring. It was only a matter of time before you were found. Now that you have awakened to Sight, it is no doubt that if you were hidden from him before, you no longer are. He wants to use you, with hope that you have inherited the advanced talents from your mother. Mix that with your Demon blood and the barriers between realms become nonexistent for you. If he can get to you, and convince you to join his side, he will use you and your gifts to spread the demonic entities like a true plague across the realms."

My mother knowingly had a relationship with a demon and I was half demon. This thought repeated in my mind over and over after he finished his speech. I did my best to listen uninterrupted and hold my questions for the end. But his confession was more than my mother's history. It was the end of the world; it was the last nail in the coffin that was my life. His words meant that any hope I ever had of living a life without terror was no more.

That creature that visited me in my dreams, who called me his daughter, was in fact my father. That monster was looking for me, waiting for me to join it. How in the hell could my mother ever love something like that?

The longer I sat in the thoughts, the more muffled they become until my mind and body were numb. I'd asked him for his knowledge,

58

demanded it even, but I wanted nothing more than for him to take it all back.

"What does this mean for me? What am I supposed to do?" I stared at him through eyes clouded with tears.

"Come with me. Join us. We can protect you." He nodded with a small sympathetic smile.

"Who is 'us' and why should I trust you? How do I know you aren't one of my daddy's demon minions? I mean, it was you who fucked up my car." I needed to know that I could trust him. My gut told me I could, but I no longer trusted the guidance of my gut, not that I ever listened to it, anyway.

"It was necessary, I apologize for that. I already have someone who is going to pick it up and repair what I did, and all the other things that clearly need mechanical attention. I'll have it dropped off at your place in a couple days." The judgement in his tone wasn't because I was the spawn of a demon, but because I hadn't taken proper care of my ride. Men.

"I was getting to all of those things. You didn't have to do that."

"Look, Josephine, I know that this is a lot to take in. You must have a ton of questions for me. I don't blame you for not being able to process your thoughts right now, but I swear to you, all that I say is the truth. The world is unraveling. You have a choice in front of you. You will either be the thread that keeps that from happening or the one that will ensure that it does."

"Take me home. Please."

As we drove in silence, I thought about returning to my tiny apartment and climbing into my bed. That was all I wanted. To forget not only what Sam had revealed to me, but his entire existence. I could find comfort in my bed, that was until my eyes closed and sleep captured my mind. I was certain that just like every night before that one, he would visit. My dearest demon daddy.

It wasn't until Sam spoke that I realized my focus had been on the rhythmic patterns of his breathing. The deep rise and fall of his chest, the passage of air through his lungs, I could hear it all and it drowned out my thoughts. My mind was a terrible place for refuge.

"Are you okay?" He touched my hand on the armrest between us. His touch was light, testing my limits before his fingers latch firmly around my own.

"No, I'm not okay. How can I be after all that has happened, after all that you have told me?" The tears returned to blur my vision and I dropped my head back on the seat.

"Is there anything I can do for you?" He studied me carefully. "I'll do whatever you need to help you get through this."

"Yes, to be honest there is. Come up there with me. Sit next to me and say nothing. Just breathe, and stay here with me, through the night. Can you do that?" I meant the question as a test and expected him to deny me and to insist that I needed time to myself to process what was happening.

"Yes, I can do that for you." His cool response was a face that came without hesitation.

He was already out of the car before I could tell him I wasn't seriously asking him to come into my home. He opened my door and held his hand out to me, and it hit me that my request wasn't just a test. I didn't want to be alone that night. I accepted his offer in hand. I calculated the realness of Sam, the warmth, the texture, the pulse beneath his flesh, and I understood just how lost I was.

Edward had been my only companion for weeks. He provided a simulated experience of connection, but touching him, being near him, felt nothing like it did with Sam.

I apologized to Sam because the elevator was still out of commission and we'd be hiking it up the stairs. This was yet another opportunity for him to bail on the commitment, yet he stayed true to his word.

We'd hit the fourth floor when the sharp pain started at my temple. The pain was familiar, the same clawing sensation that happened whenever I denied a soul. I hadn't even encountered one that day, and

60

yet there it was. I touched my eyes, nose and mouth, expecting blood. There was none.

The pain grew so intense that I stopped climbing the steps and clutched Sam's arm. At the landing of the fifth floor, my legs gave way, and I released my grip on him to press my hands against the sides of my head. The excruciating cry released from my own lips and bounced back to me in echoes throughout the stairwell. My pleads for release did nothing to stop the searing pain in my head, the tremors of my body, or the lack of control over my limbs.

"Are you okay?" Sam positioned himself in front of me to stop me from tumbling down the stairs. A cautious glance allowed him to assess my condition before he lifted me into his arms. "What is your apartment number?"

It took three attempts before he could understand my apartment number between my cries of pain. The stairwell and hallway were too public. It wouldn't be long before nosey neighbors were peeking out to see who is causing the disruption.

Already, Mrs. Crathers, a small bobble sized woman, had her head poked out of her door as we reached my floor. She shot a questioning look at Sam, who smiled and reported that I had one too many drinks at a party we never attended. Her disgusted scoff held all the judgement of the old and bitter. What I'm sure were curses from the old hag, were spat at us. She slammed her door to add to the disapproval.

Same only had minimal struggles as he work to balance my weight and open the door to my apartment. Inside, he easily navigated the space, and gently placed me on the bed. After he made sure I was comfortable he retrieved a glass of water from the kitchen to sit on the nightstand beside me. Instead of leaving, he pulled the small chair from the dining table and sit next to the bed.

"You're really going to stay here with me?" He had a clear chance to escape, but he didn't take it.

"Look, I know you don't know much about me, but I'm not one to break a promise." He leaned back in the chair. "Now you wanted us to sit in silence. Be quiet and rest."

A half hour since our graceful entrance, the clawing pain in my head eased. Sam remained by my side as promised. Concerned with my raising temperature, he'd retrieved a cool towel from the bathroom which he'd refreshed twice already. He watched over me quite like Edward had, but this was different. When his hand brushed against my face as he replaced the towel, he felt real. The deep rise and fall of his chest matched my own, because unlike the ghost he stood in for, Sam still breathed air.

I watched him just as intently as he did me and when my eyelids grew heavy, I fought the weight of them.

"Please, Josephine, get some rest." Sam nodded. "I'll stay here as long as you like, but you need to rest."

"Are you sure?"

"Again, I'm a man of my word. I'll be here."

I nodded, accepting his promise, and within moments, drifted to sleep.

My dream was different for the first time since I started spending my nights with Edward. I was in my childhood bedroom. Sports memorabilia lined the walls and shelves. My trophies from basketball, track, and soccer stood prominently on the shelves. On my bed was the first purse I ever owned, a gift from my mother when I turned sixteen.

I remembered this day. I'd laid it across the bed as I prepared for my first official date with Thomas J. The small black handbag with a checkered pattern lay next to the matching dress my mom picked out. Black with lace, not my style, but it made my mama happy, so I wore it.

The hinges on the door creaked as the door opened and in walked the woman I thought I would never see again. I thought I was reliving a fantasy until I saw the look on her face. It wasn't that of a mother entering the room ready to help her daughter prepare for a night out with a cool guy. It was a mother who hadn't seen her daughter in years and expected to never see her again.

"Mom?" I wanted it to be her, stranger things had definitely happened.

"Joey, baby, oh how I have missed you!" She pulled me into her

62

arms and peppered my cheeks with kisses.

This is really happening, isn't it? This isn't a dream. You're actually dead, but I'm still here with you." My response was a mixture of a groan and a laugh, because how much more insane could my life possibly get?

"Yes. This is happening and I'm so sorry." She released me and stepped back. There was sadness in her eyes and worry that doesn't belong. Her soul deserved to rest peacefully, away from the troubles of the world. But the crease of her brow is enough to know that she wasn't kicking it in paradise.

"What do you have to be sorry for?" Eagerly I engaged yet another hug because she was my mom and it had been too long since I felt her love wrapped around me. How could I not take advantage of the moment?

"I'm sorry for bringing you into this life." She sniffled, and tears showed on the brim of her lids.

"You're sorry I was born?" I scoffed and poked at her. A joke to lighten the mood and she actually smiled. A small one, but it was there.

"No, child, it was never my hope for you to have the same burden as I did. Sight is no gift, though that's exactly how they try to sell it to you. I'm sorry for who your father is, and I'm sorry for the life that the universe is about to force on you simply because of the terrible decisions that I've made." She hugged me again, and this time her arms linger around me.

"Oh, that, well, no biggie, Mom." My smile was for her. To let her know that I loved and missed her. The last thing I wanted her to spend her afterlife doing was worrying about me.

"I wish that were true." She looked at my hair, or lack thereof, and shook her head.

"So, Mom, you fell in love with a demon. Tell me, how does that happen?" The mood was not one I wanted to live in. Here I was, with a rare opportunity to speak to my mother after they took her from me. Life happened along with all the things we wished we could change. Moments

JESSICA CAGE

like that, those precious extractions of time, were to be cherished. How many people would ever get to see a loved one after losing them from the physical world?

"Naiveté, that's how that happens. I believed that he was different. I believed that he believed it too and that he could change what he naturally was. We both found out the hard way that that isn't possible. Eventually, no matter how hard he tried to outrun it, it all came out. That darkness that held claim to his soul, it took over him. When it did, after being denied for so long, it was fierce and terrifying and there was no getting him back.

"I had no choice but to run. However, it wasn't as simple as breaking up. Getting away from him was so much more complicated. He would never have allowed me to leave him, not with you. I had to trick him, I had to go on the run and lead him through the planes until he followed me into the Lighted. It's a realm where things of darkness are neutralized. They lose their powers there. I had to trap him there and with the help of others with Sight, I managed to do that."

"So, locked away is good, but if he is neutralized and powerless, how is he suddenly contacting me?"

"You're with Sight now. Because of recent events, the barriers between the realms are weaker. I'm not sure how, but I felt the change. We all did. Your father has figured out a way to leave the Lighted realm. I have no doubt that he found help through other demons. He had quite a following. When he finally accepted the darkness inside of him, he was phenomenal. If only he would have used that to benefit good. Instead, he grew darker and darker, until the man I loved no longer existed."

"So, demon dad is coming for me, because life just wasn't complicated enough. Not with an almost boyfriend who happens to be a ghost and now Sam telling me that I need to come and join the other members of the Sighted community as if I didn't already have a life of my own."

"Joey, I know this is a lot, but you're a strong woman. You always have been." My mom will never pander to me. She wouldn't offer me false comfort like I was a child. She never did. I loved and missed that about her.

64

"Yeah, I know, Mama, it's just a lot to take in." I flopped down on my bed and the scent of roses wafted up from the comforter. My mother had a habit of spraying the bedding with rose water. I would have to do it myself. "What do you think I should do? I mean, I know what I should do, but I don't know if I want to do it."

"Go with Sam, Joey. Let that man help you." Plain and simple, it's the obvious choice to make. It's also the choice I was hoping to avoid.

"Can't you just help me instead? If that were an option, my mother would have offered it up, but it wasn't. It was a gift enough that she could visit me in the dream.

"No, I have left your plane and I can no longer return there. Death for the Sighted is different, but now, you can visit me when you need me. I am always here."

"Thanks, Mom. I love you, and I miss you so much." We embraced once more, and her shoulder muffled my sobs. I wanted more time, more moments to add to my collection, but the nagging feeling of a dream ending pulled me from her. I'd return. She said I could if I needed to.

Awaking from my visit with Mama, I am met with an awkwardly positioned man who kept his promise. His body hung around the chair sloppily as he struggled to find comfort. He failed, obviously. The sunlight reached through the window behind his head. The glow that the halo gave to his skin took me back to one of my favorite moments with my mother.

My toes were buried deep in the sand and she danced through the water, kicking and splashing against the waves.

"Sam?" I tapped his knee and sat up from the bed.

"Yes?" He grunts as he awakened, and I laughed as he wiped the small trail of drool away from his chin.

"Thanks for staying with me." I hand him a tissue from the nightstand. "I really appreciate it."

"No problem, I hope it helped." He stood from the chair, unfolding the length of his body, and stretched. The elevation of his arms lifted his shirt revealing the bottom pair of what I imagined was a six-pack and my thoughts went right back to a place they had no business being.

"It did, it really did. I haven't been sleeping all that well." I stand from my bed and put a few steps between us. I need the space for my own sanity. "You know, you could have moved to the couch. That had to be uncomfortable for you."

"Good. So, what now?" He clapped his hands together and a massive smile stretched across his face. I hadn't even agreed to let him mentor me on the ways of the Sighted, and yet there he was, ready and willing.

"Now? Now you tell me more about the Sighted. Now, I swallow my pride and allow you to help me. But first, how does a round of pancakes sound?" I stood and our bodies were so close that he stumbled and tripped over the chair.

"Sounds good." He tried to recover from the embarrassment, but the damage was done.

I used the time it took me to whip up a mountain of pancakes and eggs to compile a mental checklist of questions I wanted to be answered. Sam retreated to the couch after grabbing a cup of coffee. He planted himself in front of the television, scanning the news channels.

Every so often, he would groan as something flashed across the screen that displeased him. I never asked him what was upsetting him because I really didn't want to know. There was already so much we needed to discuss. Adding more to that list was a waste of valuable time. When the food was ready for consumption, I fixed our plates and set up the table.

"You ready to eat?" I asked and handed him a fork as he joined the table.

"Mmm, smells good." He rubbed his stomach and pulled up the chair that had nearly taken him out. "Thank you, it's very kind of you to do this."

"Well, it's the least I could do to repay you. I mean, to thank you for staying with me last night. I'm not sure what happened, but I have a feeling it would have been worse if I were alone." I worked to cut my pancakes into bite-sized pieces.

"You asked, so yeah, I had to." He took one complete pancake, rolled it up, dipped it in the syrup he poured onto his plate, and stuffed the entire thing into his mouth.

"There is more if you like." I pointed to the stove where the excess meal waited. It wasn't unlike me to cook enough food for a small basketball team whenever dealing with stress. It was better than binging. Usually, by the time I finished cooking all the food, my desire to consume it would be non-existent. I'd end up either giving it to one of the many bachelor buddies I had, or if I were going into the city the next day, I'd make meals for the homeless man who slept just beyond the exit to my train station.

"Oh, good. Sorry, I'm starving. I haven't eaten a thing since yesterday morning unless you count the bite-sized Snickers I found in my glove compartment." He stood from the table with his plate in hand, which is still half-full, and retrieves the extra eggs and pancakes from the stove. He left nothing behind. He returned to the table with a toothy smile and hungry eyes. Sam devoured three more pancakes and half the bowl of eggs before I began my interrogation.

"I saw my mom last night while I was sleeping," I admitted before sipping the warm coffee. "It was a dream but felt like something more."

"That is good." He sipped the offered orange juice, nodding in recognition of the event I spoke of. "That means you're on the right path now. Others have had the same experience."

"Have you?" It wasn't a question I prepared to ask, but it was one I wanted him to answer.

"No, at least not anyone as significant." He leaned back with a sausage in his hand. "I used to get visits from one of my great ancestors. I didn't know the man in life, he'd died about 100 years before I was born. But he offered me guidance when I needed it. It's been years since we've last met."

"So, the connection ends?"

"Eventually, yes."

"I'll take it, considering most nights it has been my demonic daddy visiting me. Why was it different last night?"

"The only thing that has changed is my presence, an easy assumption would be the environmental shift. That and the fact that I relayed a bit of information about your past before you fell asleep. Perhaps those two factors allowed you to connect with her. Perhaps it opened you up to the possibility of seeing her again. I know how you felt about the afterlife prior to all that has recently happened in your life. Just because you did what they requested of you to avoid the physical consequences doesn't mean that you actually accepted all that it implies."

"How could you possibly know how I felt about anything? I haven't told you anything about me or my beliefs."

"It's my job. You wished for no afterlife, no chances of rekindling any lost relationships or being responsible for another existence. If there is no afterlife, there is no one waiting for you. All of this goes against everything you believed." He glanced quickly at the muted television and sighed. "You know most of the people we help, they're just like you. They don't want to believe there is anything after this. We help them accept what is waiting for them."

"She said I should go with you, and that I should trust you. I love my mom and respect her wishes, but I cannot just run off with you without being sure that it makes sense for me. The more you say, the less sense it makes." His insight into my life and the thoughts I never spoke had my stomach twisted into knots. There was something more to Sam, something he wasn't sharing with me. How could he know so much about me and yet, we'd never shared a single moment together?

"Well, I'm an open book. I know you want me to make it make sense. That is not something that will come easy. What I can tell you is that every question I answer will only give birth to more in your mind."

"I know, you're right." I pushed my plate aside. "Just tell me everything you can. I know I'll only have more questions, but I need to make an informed decision about what to do from here."

"Understood." He straightened in the chair, scoffed down the last of his food and orange juice and began, "The Sighted have been around since the beginning. We guide lost souls to be judged. It is not our job to place judgement or to interfere with whatever is to come for them. It's our responsibility to keep the natural balance of the planes."

"The balance of the planes? What planes?"

"There are celestial planes that exist between life and death, good and evil. Everything rests on a giant balancing board that must stay even. If it tilts too far in either direction, there will be complete chaos. I know what you're thinking. If it goes a little further in the odds of good, it won't hurt anything. But that just isn't true. Demons weren't the only ones trying to snag a few extra souls. Angels had their hands in the cookie jar as well, but if either side should manage to disrupt the balance, all hell would be unleashed on Earth."

"And souls are the key to that balance. What are they, like currency?"

"They are more like an energy source. The more souls either side has, the more power they have. This is why we must do our jobs, and why there are painful consequences when we choose not to."

"Right, the consequences, not fun at all." I cringed as I remembered the old woman who had attacked me in the parking lot outside of my apartment. It wasn't like I could ever forget her mangled form. "The pain and the blood, it was terrible."

"The bleeding and pain are nothing in comparison to what they are capable of. That is just the beginning. If you encounter a spirit, a soul that is strong enough, they can actually cause you to live through the agony of their own death. I had the misfortune of experiencing that once myself. It was a guy who had gotten run down by a bus. He scared the shit out of me when he came up to me. All I wanted was to get away, but I was frozen. I couldn't force my limbs to move. The closer he got to me, the more consumed I was by the fear of him. My mind went blank until he touched me, and I could feel the exploding impact of the bus hitting me. I felt my bones crush and the tires rolling over my chest. It was terrible. He felt so much pain. I wouldn't wish that on anyone."

"I'm sorry you had to go through that. I haven't experienced anything as involved as that." I allowed him a chance to recollect himself from the memory before I continued. "What else can you tell me?"

"Well, I can tell you that most of this stuff you will learn as we go. There is a community of people waiting for me to bring you back. The balance that we are supposed to protect is in serious danger of being thrown off and as much as I hate to tell you this, they're looking at you to fix it. You will have a lot more put on your shoulders than perhaps you want to deal with, more than any person should. It's unfair, and I totally expect you to run from it. I know I would if I were in your shoes, but the only way we will know any of this for sure is if you come with me."

He cleaned his fingers by licking them clean. Our eyes met as he reached his thumb, sucking the syrup from his flesh and the tension flooded the room. My thighs pressed tighter together, and my pulse raced. How could I really be ready to pounce across the table at a man who had just finished telling me that my life was over?

He wanted to take me away from my home, to a place unknown, filled with people who wanted me to save the world. It was completely unnerving and yet all I could think about was the way his jeans cupped his ass, the movement of the muscles beneath his shirt with each deep rise and fall of his chest, and wishing he was licking me instead of his thumb.

"Okay, let's do this." I took a deep breath and pushed away from the table.

"You're coming with me?" He feigned surprise but he knew exactly what my response was going to be. What other choice did I have?

"Yes. Balance of the universe is on the line, right? I can be selfish but not enough to say fuck the world. Just let me pack a small bag or something."

"Josephine?"

"Yes?" I stopped my hunt for the duffle bag I purchased for the gym I visited twice in two years.

"I know this is a lot to take on, and it might not mean much to you, but I'm proud of you."

"Thanks," I nodded and pointed to the food on my plate. "Now finish up, I saw you eyeing my eggs."

I hadn't put one thing in the bag before he'd emptied the plate.

CAMPOUT

For the third time in less than twelve hours, I climbed into Sam's car. My brain worked to comb through all the information he provided over breakfast, a process that was only halted by my struggle to pack my things. Sure enough, one planned bag turned to four, a change I rationalized because I didn't know how long I'd be away.

I couldn't decide on the necessities, so I stuffed a little of everything in the bags. Sam told me it was unnecessary, but he was a man, how could he know what I needed? In addition to the clothes, devices, and hygiene products, I packed my camera. A quick email to my boss gave me the approval I needed to work remotely. Most of my job was performed out of the office, so it wasn't that difficult to justify.

Though relieved she approved my request, I questioned how long her patience would last before she grew tired of my circumstances. Despite everything that was happening in my life, I wasn't ready to give up on my dreams. There had to be a way to find balance.

Sam's bellowing laughter as we carried my haul down the stairs, had once again called my nosey neighbors to place their judgment. The little old hags would have a field day discussing my recent antics. They even watched from their windows as we loaded the car. With my bags are stored away in the trunk and across the back seat, my mind returned to the task at hand, figuring out what my next move was.

The drive took us further south, away from the city and into the rural counties. The day was warm, so I opened the window to enjoy the scent of the land. We hadn't made it very far from home and yet this air was fresher and easier to breathe. It was easy to forget how beautiful Illinois was. Living in and around Chicago, all I knew was the crowded ways of the city. When my mother was alive, we would escape into nature. The past few years, working the agonizing day job, I hadn't had much time to explore the world. My job as a photographer was going to allow me that opportunity.

The drive offered the chance to capture landscapes of empty plains, herds of cattle, and rundown barns. Sam laughed when I forced him to pull over because he'd placed my camera bag in the trunk and I just had to take photos. He was patient, however, while I worked to capture the image of a cow with her heifer.

I'd fallen asleep, lulled by the vibration of the engine, and woke up to the jostling effect of tires over rocks. We were no longer on the open road but driving through unfamiliar woods. Just as I parted my lips to question our route, he brought the car to a stop.

"We hike from here." His plastered grin served no purpose but to mock me.

"Hike?" Instead of complaining, which was exactly what he expected, I shrugged. "Good thing I'm a nature girl. I'm sure I packed my boots somewhere." I leaned into the back seat to dig through the black duffel bag and came back.

"Good, you're going to need them."

I switched the sporty flats for the boots and froze. "Wait, what about my stuff?"

He slapped the steering wheel with shoulder bounding laughter. "I told you to pack light." He jumped from the car and heads to the trunk.

"You know you could have told me we would be trekking through the woods." I tied the boots and joined him behind the car.

"I told you not to pack so much." He handed me an empty backpack. "You didn't want to listen to me."

"What am I supposed to do with this?"

"Fill it with whatever you think will be useful." He shrugged. "We'll be gone for a couple of days at least."

"And you're just going to leave the car here?"

"No one will bother it."

"How do you know?"

"Being Sighted comes with extra talents. Not only can you see things others cannot, but you can control what others see." He slapped the side of the car.

"Meaning?" I unzipped the bag and chewed on the idea of filling it.

"Anyone without the gift of Sight, won't be able to see the car."

"Oh, can I do that?"

"You will be able to once you hone your skills."

It took me half an hour, but I got it all down to two manageable bags that I strapped to myself along with my camera case because I went nowhere without my camera. The woods would offer a ton of beautiful sights that I would want to capture. Hopefully something I could send to my boss.

"You ready to roll?" I ask him as I secure the last of my gear and smile.

"Yeah." He nudged me on the shoulder. "Let's hit it."

"So where exactly are we going?" I asked, stopping to take a picture of small black birds nesting on a low branch.

"We're going to see Orion. She's something like an oracle for our kind." He kept moving ahead, refusing to wait for me.

"Okay," I caught up with him. "What are you hoping she will do? Is she going to tell me my future?"

"I'm hopeful she'll have some insight on what our next step

should be. With your father on the rise along with his demons, we need to be sure that we're doing whatever it takes to keep him from succeeding." He slowed his pace as he reached a particularly rough patch of terrain.

"Will she be able to tell us how to defeat them?"

"She cannot tell us how to succeed, only if success is possible." He grabbed my hand to help me across a fallen tree. "If we're lucky, she'll give us a few cryptic hints to decipher. That's the most we can hope for. If she says too much, she risks altering the course of things and changing the future."

"A full blueprint would be nice, but I'll take whatever I can get."

"You get used to it." He studied the path ahead of us. "Besides, you've been around ghosts long enough to know how they speak. This won't be much different."

The further we walked; the more frustrated Sam got. Multiple times he prodded me to move faster, but I ignored his agitations. Admittedly, it wasn't only because I wanted to capture the wonders of nature or because I enjoyed aggravating him so much, which was a great perk. I wasn't in a hurry to meet this Orion or any of the other Sighted ones. I was walking into a pit of fire and each step further was another step closer to the burn.

Don't get me wrong, I wanted to understand all the madness, but even with that understanding it wouldn't change the way I felt. I didn't want any of it. Nothing would have been better than returning to my simple existence with my uncomplicated life goals.

"We will have to set up camp," Sam announced as we hit another rough patch of land. "No way we're going to make it across this before nightfall."

"What?" I looked ahead. The ground would be tough to cross, but it didn't appear to be that bad. "Don't tell me you're afraid of the dark. If you're too tired, you can admit it. I won't tell anyone I outlasted you!"

"I know you would enjoy the bragging rights, but that's not the issue here. We need to take cover, nightfall is coming, and this is not the place to be wandering around in after the sun goes down." He scouted the area. "We should find a secure place to set up for the night."

After ten minutes of thoughtful searching, he settled on a small space tucked away inside the foliage. It wasn't an ideal location. On uneven ground and hidden away from the beautiful night sky that we'd apparently be missing out on. Despite my concerns, he was adamant that the spot he'd chosen was perfect.

"We don't need a panoramic view, we need protection."

"It's not as if there are bears out here," I mutter as I pitched the tent he provided.

While I struggled with his simplistic tent, he gathered firewood. We were in the middle of summer and he was gathering firewood. The last few nights were scorchers, and the forecast called for another terrible heatwave, but again he insisted.

"Hidden protection and firewood? Is all this really necessary?" I questioned when he returned with an armful of wood.

"Josephine, can you please just trust that I know what I'm talking about?"

"No, I can't. I have the right to ask you questions, Sam. I'm not just going to accept whatever you tell me without considering the logic behind it. If you want me to blindly follow you, we can turn around right now."

"You're right. I'm sorry, I'm just frustrated." He dropped the wood and wiped the sweat from his brow. "You're different now. Your experiences will be too. Your life, the rules that you were used to playing by, they aren't the same." He kicked the collected pile, and the logs scattered. "This is exactly why you should have been with us and not with that damn ghost!"

"That's a cheap shot." I continued my fight with the tarp covering.

"Again, I apologize." He watched without so much as an offer of help.

"I know you don't like him, but that's no reason to be an ass about it," I muttered as the pole fell and hit my toe for the third time.

"I don't like him, that's true." He retrieved the pole and handed it back to me. "But that's not the problem here."

"Then what is?"

"Your relationship with him. It's not right."

"So, you've expressed." I gave up my struggle with the tent.

"Leave it, I'll do it."

"I'm capable of putting a tent together."

"Clearly, you're doing an outstanding job," he snickered.

"Do you have a problem with me?"

"Yeah, you walk slow, take too many pictures, and you have a bug on your forehead." He pointed to my head.

"I what?"

"There is a bug, a beetle, I think, on your forehead."

"What?!" I nearly fell on my ass trying to flick the invader off my forehead. A false step had my foot twisted in the tent ropes, but thanks to his quick reflexes, I landed in the secure hold of his arms.

"I think you got it."

"Whatever," I huffed as he placed me on my feet. "Put the tent together."

"Right away, Dear." The man laughed about the damn bug the entire time he worked on his ridiculous tent.

"You got any food?" My stomach growled as I watched a small squirrel run by with a hand full of seeds.

"Yeah, there are some sandwiches on the bottom of my backpack."

"Sandwiches?"

"I grabbed a few subs while you were sleeping on the drive up." He grabbed the bag and pulled out the wrapped sandwiches. "I hope turkey is okay."

"Yes, perfect, thank you!"

"There's one for you and two for me, by the way." He put the last touches on the tent and lit the fire before sitting next to me.

"You work up a hunger fast." I laughed as he rushed to clean his hands with the wet wipes and devoured the first sandwich.

"Hey, I did a lot of walking." He took another hearty bite. "I also had to gather the wood and put the tent up by myself."

"I helped."

"Helped make it more complicated." He pointed at the structure beneath the low-hanging branches. "How did you manage to get the rope wrapped around the branch like that?"

"If you got an updated tent, that wouldn't have happened." I handed him a napkin to wipe the food from his mouth. "You know, I'm not going to steal your food. You can take your time."

"Not my fault you're a lady. Women can't be piggish, at least not in front of the general male population." Making animalistic grunts, he retrieved two bottles of water from his bag and tossed one to me.

"It's going to be a beautiful night," it was best to ignore his last statement. We'd argued enough for one day, and the topic of his sexism would only lead to another lengthy debate. I would not apologize for eating like a civilized person.

"For now." A chill passed through my bones with the ominous tone of his words.

"What does that mean? You think that it will change?" I cracked open my water and took a slow swallow of the cool liquid. The surrounding air dropped in temperature, adding to the effect to his statement. I inched closer to the fire and received a raised brow from my cocky companion.

"Always does." His relaxed demeanor turned serious as he watched the changing sky. "This place, it's different, Josephine. In a matter of hours, it will change, and it won't exactly be safe for us to be out here, which is why I chose a spot where we can still be hidden. There are things, elements that awaken out here when the sun goes down."

"Ghosts?"

"Yes, there will be ghosts and other things. This land is one of the access points, a gateway between the planes. We may see things; unnatural things cross us. But no matter what you see tonight, stay hidden, whatever you do, don't draw attention to our location. As long as we stay covered and in the shadows, we'll have no problems. You can sleep and I will keep watch until dawn. Then, once you are awake, and the danger is gone, I'll get some rest before we proceed."

"You expect me to be able to sleep knowing that there will literally be ghouls and goblins walking around me?" I gathered and bagged our trash. "No thank you, I will be up with you. Sleep at dawn sounds fine."

"Are you sure?"

"Yes. As you said, there is a lot that I will learn in practice. I need to see this, especially since I'm expected to travel across these planes the same way my mother could do. It might help to get a glimpse at what to expect if I should ever be able to perform such a task." I wanted to see what happened, that was the entire point of my agreeing to go with him.

There were so many unknowns that affected my life. Every day another issue revealed itself. Every time I looked up there was more that left me confused and afraid. This would be an observation, nothing more. At least for once, I wouldn't be the subject of discovery.

The sky continued to darken, and the temperature dropped. We occupied ourselves with conversations about things both extraterrestrial and not. He spilled the beans about the famous people who had the gift of Sight. The politicians, actors, and musicians who work to keep our world at peace and in balance. The most shocking revelation had to be a major pop star that had recently suffered a mental breakdown which left her swinging from chandeliers with her crotch showing. Sam shrugged her actions away and called them an unfortunate side effect of having her eyes opened to her true purpose. Everyone coped in different ways.

"Do you mean to tell me I might start dressing weird and twerking on teddy bears?"

"Oh yeah, you may even decide to take the path of Lady Gaga... meat suits!" His loud laughter shots shorts with the sound of something fast approaching. "Come on, into the tent," Sam waved me toward the safe space. I did as he asked. He stamped out the last of our fire just as the beast rushes by our space.

"What the hell was that?" I pulled him closer to me in the tent and whispered as low as I could.

"That was one of the lost. Spirits who hold such attachments to earth that they are unable to leave no matter who tries to take them. We call them Windlins because to most people, the ones without sight, they're just strong gusts of wind. A little literal, but it works." He adjusted himself inside the tent and closed the opening as much as he could. "They're mostly harmless, but don't underestimate them. If they feel threatened, they will attack. If they do attack, they will pull a part of your soul into them. It works as sort of a tag, a marking on your soul that promises you the same endless existence when you die." He pulled two blankets out of the bag tucked at the back of the tent and wrapped one around me before using the other to cover just his legs.

"So that was just a normal Earth spirit, not something that crossed over from another plane?" My throat tightened. That was considered the pleasant side of the creatures we might encounter.

To call an entity that possessed the ability to doom someone to endless insanity was a joke. Fortunately, the rest of the night was eventless. We sat and waited but witnessed nothing more than the scurrying of local wildlife.

Though we saw nothing, we heard more than enough. There were howls, growls, and deadly moans amplified from all angles. I did as Sam instructed. I remained as quiet and as motionless as possible. The night was long, tense, and just before dawn, unnervingly silent. I finally slip into a soft slumber as the sun peeked over the horizon and Sam

80

assured me it was safe.

ORION

We walked for about two hours after waking from our brief nap. I expected to be exhausted after the lack of sleep, but oddly, I had enough energy to spare. I snapped a few more pictures that I thought my boss would love and continue to move forward. This time I didn't lag. After spending the night in the ghost-filled woods, I wanted to meet Orion. She knew what was ahead of me, and I needed her to tell me all that she could. There were too many things in the world that I was blind to and that number of unknowns was only expanding.

"We're here." Sam stopped at a small stream of water pouring from the mouth of a cave. The presence of the stream baffled me. We were in the middle of a forest near no major body of water, and yet it poured endlessly and ended in nothing. There was no pool of water, no pond to wade through to reach its entrance.

I followed his footsteps climbing through the flow and into the cave. When we crossed the barrier of the cave's entrance, there was no water on the opposite side.

"What's up with the freaky water effect?" I asked him as he slowed his pace.

"I have no idea, ambiance?" He chuckled. "It's never the same when you come here. Orion like to change things up a bit."

Tucked away in the back of the cave was a small door drawn into the stone. Sam turned to me and placed his index finger over his lips, showing that it's best that I not speak. I held my breath as if that would make me any more inaudible. He knocked twice and whistled a soft melody. Then knocked twice more and spoke a rhyme too quickly for me to comprehend, but it was something pertaining to the wind. One more knock and he said, "I am Sighted; therefore, I see." He stepped back, winked at me, and waited.

Moments later the wall dissolved, and a door formed of shadows emerged. Sam reached back, grabbed my hand, and pulled me forward with him as he passed through the shadow. For the most terrifying thirty seconds of my life, we were in complete darkness. Things moved around me. Long, sticky fingers reached out for and grabbed my legs. I wanted to scream when something sharp dug into my leg, but I kept my mouth shut, even as the warmth ran down my skin. I only hoped it wasn't my blood.

I tightened my grip around Sam's hand; he squeezed back and reassured me we would be okay. But he too remained silent. When the light returned, we were inside another cave, but one that was much larger. I looked down at my leg. No cut, no blood. I was okay; we were okay.

When my pulse calmed, I could better observe the space. There were paintings and carvings in the stone walls and unexpected modern elements like amps, computers, and a big plush couch in the center of the space. This Orion lived in style.

Sam smiled at me, and once again placed his finger over his lips. He wore a priceless expression of excitement. Whatever was about to happen was something he'd apparently looked forward to. All I could think of was how I wanted things to go well with the oracle. I could share in his excitement later if she didn't tell me to expect to end up like the Windlins.

"Sammy? You're back!" A deep, motherly voice erupted from the ceiling and rained down on us.

The droplets of sound turned into a mist that filled the room. With a loud suctioning sound, a force pulled each drop to a center, and a figure forms in front of us. Well above six feet, the woman was gorgeous.

She had a low-cut afro, dark brown skin, and the oddest shade of reddish-brown eyes I have ever seen. Her smile was enormous with a slight gap and her body was thin yet curvy. She stepped to Sam and hugged him tightly. Friends who haven't seen each other in a while.

"Nice to see you too, O," He pulled back from the embrace. "I brought someone for you to meet. I believe you have been waiting for her arrival."

"Ah, yes, Ms. Josephine." Her long arms pulled me into her and wrapped so far around me she touched herself on either side of my smaller frame. With my arms pinned to my side, there was nothing I could do but ride out the embrace. The hug lasted a bit longer than I would have preferred, but I didn't want to offend her.

"Hello," I squeak out just before she released me, "it's nice to meet you."

"It's about damn time you made your way over here. Girl, the hype, the talk, the rumors, the tales, you have no idea how many times my ear has been talked off about you. People are so nosy. 'Has she come yet? Is she the one?' Child, I am exhausted just from the questioning alone!" She talks without so much as a single breath as she walks to a side table that holds various bottles of liquor. Some I recognize and others I wouldn't try if you paid me. "You want some?" She held a gold glass bottle out to me and offered me a sample of the brown sludge inside.

"No thank you." I politely rejected the drink.

"Well, more for me. Trust me, you'll be begging me for it later." She laughed and the sound reverberated throughout the cave. The large woman had a personality twice her size. "I guess we should just get this thing done. The anticipation will kill me! Oh, and we have to be sure to get you two back to your plane before the sun goes down. Don't want to be stuck in my world at night, gets real freaky around here." She leaned into me with a sly wink.

I couldn't tell if she meant freaky as in scary or freaky as in kinky. Either way, I refused to ask for clarification. It might be something harmless, but just in case it was more menacing, I'd like to avoid it at all costs. She could have just been a freak who intended on having a few more interesting visitors. If that were the case, we damned sure needed to get out of there as soon as possible. I was not signing up for an otherworldly orgy.

"Wait, what do you mean? We aren't on Earth?" For the first time since she appeared, I took my eyes off Orion and found Sam, pouring himself a glass of whatever the blue slime was.

"No, not exactly. The doorway I opened was just like the passageways I told you about." While his face showed no signs of emotions, his eyes betrayed his attempt to hide his enthusiasm. Of course, it excited him. Take away the threat of my dear old demonic daddy, and I might have found joy in the possibility of crossing worlds too.

"So, we have to go back the way we came." I rubbed my arms to push away the returning feeling of sticky hands that grabbed me as we passed through the dark space. "So those things..."

"Lost souls, Child," Orion offered sweetly. "They are the ones who were unfortunate enough to fall off the path between the planes. They reach for you and try to pull you in. Some say they want you to pull them out. Either way, they can't harm you as long as you stay on the path. One foot off, hell just one toe and you become one of them. Once you fall, there's no coming back." She ushered me to the couch in the center of the room.

Large nets that sparkled with firelights hung above our heads, and the scent of roses filled my head.

"Rose water?" I lifted the pillow to my face and inhaled the familiar scent.

"Oh yes, I remember your mother loved that scent, too."

"She did. She used to spray my bedding with it."

"Smart woman." She joined me on the couch. "Now, it's time for us to focus on finding out all there is to know about Ms. Josephine Massey." She claps her hands together in one loud thwack.

"What do I have to do?" My voice was a nervous rattle.

"Relax." Sam joined us on the couch and grabbed my hand in

between his own. "I'm here."

"There's nothing for you to do but sit back and try to clear your mind. The rest of the show is all me." Orion's smile was so warm the heat expanded from her heart to my own. It first touched the tip of my shoulder, then spread across the length of me. The sensation was a sensual massage that had my body melting into the couch cushions. "There, that wasn't so hard. Sam, I need you to let go of Jo. I can't have your energy mixing with hers and messing up my visions. Please go to the desk and hand me the little blue pouch from the top left-hand drawer." She directed Sam, who followed her orders and quickly retrieved the described pouch.

Orion pulled out a small glass stone that dangled from an odd-looking thread from within the pouch. The material was an etching in air. If I tried to grab it, my hand would have passed right through it. Something told me Orion was the only one capable of wielding the substance. I narrowed my eyes to get a better view of it, but it was shifty like wisps of smoke, an illusion that was hard for my vision to bring into focus.

"What is that?" My voice came as relaxed as my body felt. Each word was a long drawl that tickled my throat and lifted the corners of my lips.

"This is how I see, how I get my insight about what is coming." Orion dropped her head back as the glass stone hung between us. "Be my eyes," she whispered, and the stone swayed above me. "Let me see!" she called out. The stone moved faster, spinning wildly above me. As it moved, it picked up the light of the room, tossing it around in all directions. The stone halted and absorbed the light instead of refracting it. Orion lifted her head to reveal eyes that matched the stone. Glass orbs of light peered out at me from her dark face. "You are the one. You will bring balance, but the journey will break your soul. Your father has returned, and he is looking for you. He has one close to you. A spirit appears to be a friend, but he is not. You must sever the ties to your father. The pathways are not safe, your home, the demons, it…"

"Stop!" I heard the deep voice, familiar, before large hands grabbed Orion by the shoulder and pulled her from the couch.

"What the hell?" Edward grabbed my arm and tried to pull me

from the couch. "What are you doing here?"

"You must come with me!" His eyes bulged with terror as he searched for something I couldn't see.

"What?" My body was so still relaxed from Orion's warmth, which made standing a challenge, but I managed. I was ready to go with him, because I trusted him, but then I saw Sam also struggling to get to his feet and I knew something was wrong.

"No child, don't! He is dark; it's all over his soul!" Orion called out as she pulled herself from the floor. Her eyes still glowed with the light of the stone.

"What?" I try to help her up, but Edward's grip on my arm kept me anchored.

"Don't listen to her, Josephine. We have to go!" He yanked my arm, and the jolt caused my shoulder to pop.

"Your daddy sent him child. If you go with him, we will lose you forever!" Orion stood but kept her distance. She looked at Edward like he was the ultimate Molotov cocktail. One false move and he'd burn down the entire place.

"But that can't be true." I turned to Edward. "Tell her it isn't true." When he didn't corroborate my statement, I repeated myself. "It isn't true, is it?!"

Panic swelled in my chest as he avoided me yet again.

"Get away from her!" Sam barreled across the room and dove into Edward.

They crashed to the ground. Edward manages to get away from Sam and ran for me. Before he could reach me, Orion stepped into his path with her hand up, palm facing his chest. A bright white light shot out of her palm and into Edward. He cried out, and I moved to help him until the dark strands exited his chest where the light penetrated him.

They were coming for me, those dark tendrils. Their intentions were palpable as they followed the orders of the darkness that commanded them. Edward's eyes lock with mine and the truth is there. Frozen in my own fear, my thoughts became loud drumming. He betrayed me, lied to me. It was all true.

"No!" I heard Sam moments before his hands wrapped around the skull of Edward who clawed at him. "Back to the world where you belong!" Sam yelled, ignoring the cuts left behind on his arms by Edward's nails.

"Josephine, please." Edward reached for me one last time before he, and the strands that poured out from him vanished. Sam fell to the floor gasping for air and Orion slumped in on herself.

"Damn, that boy was strong." Orion turned to me and examined me like a broken doll.

"What the hell?" My eyes flooded with tears.

"I'm sorry, but your dad sent Edward to find you. His job was to do whatever it took to unlock your gifts," Sam spoke in a somber tone. "I suspected it, but I hoped that I was wrong. I know how much you cared about him."

All the time I'd spent with Edward, the trust I built for him, how could I have been so blind? He was closer to me than most of my friends. Knew things about me that I wouldn't dare tel anyone else. And the whole time the damn ghost boy was only there because he was paid off to be near me and to what, groom me for my father's plot?

It was a total disaster! Sam who looked like he would pass out at any moment. I considered this new man that I'd put my trust in. What if I am wrong about him as well? I couldn't take it; my body ached and my heart screamed.

What was going to happen next? How much more could go wrong? My anger was misdirected, and I allowed questions to invade my mind that only invoked more heartache. Wasn't that just the perfect invitation for disaster.

"I think I will take that drink now."

THE PHASES

"Are you okay?" Sam handed me the last water bottle and a bag of trail mix. He planned for us to make it back early enough not to need a second meal, but there was no way he could have expected how things would go with Orion.

After Edward's traumatizing exit from her layer, Orion needed time to recenter herself. She wouldn't allow us to leave until she was sure Edward wouldn't return. She added further protection to her space and before handing me a small silver necklace with a stone similar to hers fastened to it. It would protect me from Edward and any other unwanted visitors.

"I don't know, I mean how would you feel if you were in my shoes right now?"

"I have no idea." He secured the tent and checked the skyline for the fading sun. "I'll admit I judged you for being with him. Far before I knew you, but I had no idea how much you cared for him until I watched that pain in your eyes."

"Is that so wrong for me to care about a dead man?" I folded my legs into my chest and pulled the blanket tighter around my body. If I could vanish like the ghosts we ushered, Sam would have been alone in those woods. "I thought that was the point of all this. We care enough to make sure we take care of these people, of their souls. I know it was wrong, on some level, but when we were together, he wasn't the ghostly being you saw. He was real, and he made me feel safe when I was alone in this."

"I know," he took a seat next to me, covering his legs with his blanket. "I'm sorry, Josephine. Despite what I felt about any of it, you don't deserve this."

"I can't go back there, can I?" We'd taken cover again for the night. I wanted to look at the sky, stare into the dark abyss, but the sun was already too low to risk doing that. "Back to my simple apartment, my busted car, and my eventless life. He took that option away from me the second I stepped on that damn platform."

"I wouldn't say you can't ever go back. Lots of the Sighted lead normal lives."

"Right, but none of them are like me. None of them have demonic fathers hoping to use them in a plot for world domination. I do. And there is no way in hell I'm going to just go back to taking photos and making plans to move into a condo. This is my life now. Hiding in the woods hoping I don't get spotted by Windlins and I don't even want to know what else."

"This isn't your life." He shifted his weight and pushed closer to me so he could wrap one arm around my shoulder. "This is just one part of your journey. Who knows, you may defeat your father and go on to a career in chandelier swinging."

"Very funny," I smirked. My dance-challenged ass would never be able to survive a chandelier swing.

"Ah, but it got you to smile. That's a start."

"Thank you." I leaned into his warmth.

"For what?" His eyes dropped to my face.

"For the truth. As much as I hate a lot of what it revealed, I needed to know the truth."

"I wish it were all better news."

"So do I." I yawned.

"Get some rest, I'll keep watch for now." His arm tightened around me; comfort added to the moment.

"Are you sure?"

"Yeah, I suspect it will be another boring night in these ghostly woods."

Sam kept his arm around me as I allowed my mind to rest. For the first night in weeks, I had no dreams. Odd to think that the void gave me more comfort than even the visit from my mother because even she acted as a painful reminder of the irrevocable changes in my life. I was grateful for the connection to her, but if losing it meant leading a note, having to face demons and ghosts, I'd give it up.

"Get the girl!" A sharp scream woke me from my sleep. The chill of the night cut through to my bones.

"Sam?" His warmth no longer shielded me from the cold air.

"Hurry up before she gets away!" A deeper voice ordered, and I realized I was the girl they were referring to.

I stepped out of the tent just in time to avoid the ropes that wrapped around it. The force that pulled the ropes dragged it with terrifying speed through the tree line. If I'd been inside, I might have broken several bones and suffered a concussion.

"You idiot, you let her get out!" the sharper voice cried out.

These voices had no source. They carried on the air, but no matter how hard I searched, I couldn't see them. Though I had no view of their bodies, I knew their intentions. They wanted to capture me, and my gut screamed to run. I bolted in the opposite direction of the voices, calling for Sam as I ran. In hindsight, running through a ghost-infested forest screaming at the top of my lungs may not have been the best idea.

"Get down!" Startled by Sam's voice, I stopped and turned just in time to see the beast pummeling towards me.

The Windlin had its sight locked on me, but what could I have possibly done to get away from it? I couldn't outrun the wind, no matter how hard I tried.

"Move!" he yelled again and speared me. We tumbled to the ground, barely avoiding the crazed spirit.

"Run!" Sam grabbed my hand and pulled me back to my feet.

"What's happening?" Ducked down behind a massive tree, I panted to catch my breath. "Where were you?"

"Fighting to get back to you. It appears your dear old dad didn't enjoy being cut off from you."

"What?"

"That charm Orion gave you, it's working better than she thought."

"The dream." I touched the necklace hanging around my neck. "I didn't have the dream; he didn't visit me."

"Exactly. Not long after you fell asleep, those assholes arrived."

"What are they?"

"I tried to get a good look at them but judging by their shifty appearances I would say they're Phases."

"Phases?"

"Yeah, they're one of the lower demons. Not that powerful, often clumsy in their attempts to do, well, anything. I'd bet they were told to do nothing more than scout the woods for you and report back. Unfortunately, they're always trying to prove themselves, so they overreach and fuck things up."

"Okay, so clumsy demons are after us, got it." I peeked around him. "What do we do?"

"We take cover." He pointed to a massive bush. "There, we can hide in there."

"You want to hide in a bush?"

"Trust me?" He dropped to his knees and pointed to the small opening beneath the branches.

"Okay." It was either we hid in a bush, or risk the demons finding me.

Sam led the way, and I crawled into the bush behind him. Where there should have only been enough room for one person, there was enough for five or more. My skepticism instantly quieted as our crawl into the bush took us from the woods to a cozy nook. Soft fur created a barrier between my knees and the rough ground. Small floating tea lights which should have burned the bush flowed in the corners to provide light.

"What is this?" I picked up a round cushion from the corner.

"It's a budding." He checked behind me to make sure nothing entered after I did.

"A what?"

"A budding, most of the forests have them. It's a safe place to stay if you get stuck out here without provisions."

"These exist and yet we stayed in a tent?"

"They're for people who are in trouble like we are right now." He sat on one of the cushions. "If we were here and someone needed to escape a Windlin or a Phase, the budding might reject them."

"Oh."

"I know, it's a lot of rules, but once we're out of here, I'll teach you everything you need to know." He peered out the opening once again. "We should be safe now."

"Sam?"

"Yes?"

"They were going to take me to him, weren't they?"

"Yes, if they were successful, they would have dragged you back to their plane where your father awaits."

93

"What's to stop him from sending more to do the same?"

"He didn't send them. He needs you to come on your own." He pulled my hands into his. "It has to be your choice, not something forced on you. Your father knows that, and I suspect those Phases won't exist for much longer after he finds out what they've done."

"It has to be my choice?"

"Yes, as long as you choose not to go to him, and not to be on his side, he cannot win this."

"That's good. I'd never make that choice."

"I know, we just need to focus on getting you to safety. Once I make it to Solarity, you'll be safe."

"Solarity?"

"Yes, it's where the Sighted go when first introduced to this world. You'll learn to protect yourself and to hone your skills." He checked the watch on his wrist. "We still have a few hours before it'll be safe to move. Come here."

He reached for me and I returned to the safety of his hold. I closed my eyes and listened to his life. The rise and falls of this chest as he breathed, the thumping of his heart pumping blood through his veins. I absorbed his warmth and accepted his truth. Sam was real, and Real was good, it was enough.

I slipped in and out of consciousness, coaxed by the rhythm of his life, but Sam remained awake. Even after the sun rose, he powered through the hike that took us back to his car. And just as he said, the Kia waited for us, untouched.

"I can drive." I held my hand out for the keys. "You didn't get any sleep. We don't have to go far, just drive enough to get to a hotel or something. You need to rest."

He couldn't deny my reasoning. By the time we made it to the car, he was struggling to carry himself.

"Alright, there is a rest stop about ten miles from here. We can

94

hold up there."

"Good. Just point the way."

The drive was eventless, the hotel plain, but the beds were soft. We stayed just long enough for us to sleep, shower, and for me to contact my boss over the shady Wi-Fi connection. I submitted images and write-ups before I climbed into bed. I woke up to praises for my work and urges to stay away as long as I could produce the same quality. Again, I wondered how long it would be until that offer was removed from the table. I responded to her, not sure when I'd have another stable internet connection, and packed my bags.

Sam took over the drive and seven hours later we pulled off to the side of the road where there looked to be nowhere to go. He pulled a small pin from his pocket and pointed it at the lone pole that stood in front of the car.

"We're here," he looked over to me before he continued. "Are you ready for this?"

"I wish I knew how to answer that. I don't really know what to expect." The trees beyond the pole parted as we spoke and revealed a path.

"It will be easy, like starting a new school."

"Clearly you've never been the new girl joining the school in the middle of the semester. It's not a pleasant experience at all."

"It won't be that bad." He chuckled and shifted the car back into gear.

"Wait," I grabbed his hand to stop him from moving the car.

"What is it?"

"There's something I need to do first."

I removed Orion's charm from my neck and handed it to him.

"What are you doing?"

"Trust me?"

"Of course."

Outside the car, I took a deep breath. There was something else I needed to do, someone I needed to address.

"Edward?" I called out to him. He could still hear me. The moment I took the charm off, I felt the connection still there.

"I'm here." He appeared a foot away from me. "I didn't think you'd want to see me again."

"I really don't want to see you." I stepped out of arm's reach of him. "You owe me an explanation for what you did."

"I'm sorry, I am."

"I don't want your apologies, Edward, I want to know the truth."

His eyes darted to the car where Sam waited and back to me.

"Don't look at him, this isn't about him."

"What do you want to know?"

"Why did you do this to me? Why pull me into this world?"

"I had no choice."

"Edward! Stop the bullshit. Tell me the truth. Why did you do this?"

"He has her, my Delilah," he admitted.

"What?"

"Your father has her soul, trapped on his plane. He won't let her go." His voice broke as he spoke. "Not long after she stopped visiting my bench on the platform, she died. I felt it when it happened, her soul was coming to me and then, it was gone. I was waiting for her to join me." He reached into his pocket, pulling out the folded ticket. "The reason I didn't get in line like the other souls was that when I got to the courthouse, they handed me two tickets. One for me, and one for Delilah. We were supposed to leave together, only she never showed, and I cannot leave without her."

"You lied to me. This entire time, you knew what you were doing. How could you be with me, sleep with me, and know what would come?"

"None of that was supposed to happen. I didn't plan to bond with you. The connection between us was real. It still is. It's the reason I'm here now. This wasn't my doing."

"Even if you didn't plan it, you allowed it to happen. You had plenty of opportunities to tell me the truth. You could have walked away from me at any time. And yet you stayed here, with me, you climbed into my bed, you slept with me knowing that your motivation was tainted. Did you ever think to tell me the truth? Did you ever wonder if I might actually want to help you?"

"I didn't want to risk—"

"Risk what?"

"Risk losing you. You were the only one who saw me. I didn't want to leave you. I didn't want to lose the connection with you."

"You realize how selfish that is, don't you? Do you understand how angry that makes me? You chose your own happiness over mine. You wanted a connection with someone, but somehow it didn't bother you that the person on the other side of the connection was at risk? How does that work?"

"I cared; I just couldn't do anything about it."

"You had a choice; I don't care what you say. You had a choice, and you ruined everything for me. You held on to the connection but let me tell you one thing. Whatever existed between us, it wasn't real. It couldn't be, because you weren't truthful. You lied to me and broke my faith, my trust from the moment we met."

"Josephine."

"I called you here for the truth and to say goodbye, Edward." I turned and opened the door to the car.

"He won't let her go," Edward pleaded.

97

"I might have cared about that, before. I might have wanted to help you save her. But not now," I held my hand out for the stone. Sam dropped it in my hand.

"Don't do this."

I lifted the chain over my head. "I didn't do this, Edward. You did."

As the chain settled around my neck, I willed away the ghost and the connection that existed between us.

"You okay?" Sam examined my expression.

"I am now." I nodded and the car moved forward.

The ominous howling of the crazed spirit sounded as the gates to Solarity closed behind us.

About the Author

Jessica Cage is an International Award Winning, and USA Today Best Selling Author. Born and raised in Chicago, IL, writing has always been a passion for her. As a girl, Jessica enjoyed reading tales of fantasy and mystery, but she always hoped to find characters that looked like her. Those characters came few and far in between. When they did appear, they often played a minor role and were background figures. This is the inspiration for her writing today and the reason why she focuses on writing Characters of Color in Fantasy. Representation matters in all mediums and Jessica is determined to give the young girl who looks like her, a story full of characters that she can relate to.

You can also sign up for Jessica's general newsletter here.

Join Jessica Online
www.JessicaCage.com
Bookbub
Facebook
Twitter
Instagram
Tiktok

Read More of Jessica's Books
The Djinn Rebellion Series
The Siren Series
The High Arc Vampires Series
The Alphas Series
The Scorned by The Gods Series
No Love for the Wicked

Made in the USA
Columbia, SC
05 February 2024

31036465R00064